THE GIRL I KNEW

Benjamin Roberts

"There is in souls a sympathy with sounds;
And as the mind is pitch'd the ear is pleased
With melting airs, or martial, brisk, or grave:
Some chord in unison with what we hear
Is touch'd within us, and the heart replies....
With easy force it opens all the cells
Where Memory slept."

William Cowper "The Winter Walk at Noon"

For Georgiana and Derek

PROLOGUE

Sokoli - Tirana

The train creaked and clanked its way down the single track from the upper ravines to the flat Tirana plain. The old Czech engine drew dusty 1960s German carriages which were faded orange outside and had grimy warm leather seats and smelt of bleach inside. In a corner in the rear carriage, Old Sokoli kept his face turned to the hole in the broken window as the heat and smells of Tirana came in with the thick breeze. He felt in his pocket for the keys which the lawyer had sent him, making sure for the seventh time that morning that the lining in his cast-off jacket pocket had not ripped. Down the carriage, country folk sat in silence, one old woman clutching a live chicken in a plastic bag which she caressed and soothed with the fingers of her left hand, staring out the window with a slight smile, the other hand clutching her mobile 'phone. Sokoli had no 'phone. He was sure his appointment would be kept. There was no signal where he came from and he would anyway have detested being whistled for like a dog at his age. He liked the mountains.

A group of country school kids from Vora began screaming at each other as the train swayed tentatively into the one good platform, uncertain of its welcome, taking up only a small amount of the long platform with its two-carriage length, dwarfed by the five hundred yards of mighty concrete pillars which had been built to accommodate a grander railway which had never appeared and which were covered in graffiti up to shoulder-height all the way along.

Out of habit, Sokoli waited until the carriage was empty before he hoisted himself from the seat with the help of his stick and stepped backwards down the carriage-step onto the platform. He made his way up the long line of pillars to the wire fence where the brick reception hut was and went in. He paused to put his ticket down on a table in the small empty room, looking at the rows of yellowed plastic chairs which were never used but which some orderly railway soul had meticulously regimented in three straight rows and then had adorned each chair with its washed and ironed white anti-macassar. Nobody would ever notice and nobody would ever care about this small sign of order in a city which had not really changed at all in two hundred years but which was now in a chaos of new development.

Sokoli eased his way outside into the street and the raucous noise hit him, the petrol generators, one outside each shop, keeping the lights on in the drought. They had a nickname for the clatter, they called it the song of the swallows, and it came regularly in the heat of every summer when the dam up in the mountains dried out and the electricity failed. This flock of generators was perched in lines, one outside every shop, café and bar, old and new, the bare-brick and the cream marble, half-built arcades and rows of plate glass.

European cars swished along, bumping in the pot-holes in the narrow lanes left by even more cars, most stolen, some legitimate, which were jammed up against each other on the kerbs on every street. Clutching the keys in his pocket, Sokoli took his time. He tapped his way with his stick along by the bus station – full of old door-less vans bearing scribbled chalk signs of their destinations, slowly filling up with patient High Albania mountain peasants waiting for departure – only when full and not before. He thought he might have to take one of these buses back as the train had an uncertain time-table.

He walked by the rows of second-hand clothing stalls and then joined the crush of people flowing down towards Zog Boulevard and Skanderbeg Square where the big symbols of the past stood crumbling amid the beggars, carbon monoxide and frenetic building. There, as he well knew, the forgotten bronze statues of Joseph Stalin and an unknown but muscular and shapely Girl of the Revolution stood face to face and indecently close in a tryst in the shadows by the bins at the back of the National Gallery of Art. In an uncharacteristic moment of sentimentality, Sokoli had the idea that the statues waited until they could come out again, waited for the time when the disgrace had worn off and they could emerge as curiosities from the past, when the pain was long forgotten of the 40 years of repression just so recently overturned. He felt the same.

Everything he had worked for had vanished. Everything had changed. He was shocked at the sense of freedom he saw and felt in the crowds of people. Once there had only been bicycles and poverty and one idea to follow. And fear. Now there was still poverty, a few bicycles left, but there was no fear. Sokoli saw that the State Brothel had been demolished and now there was just a noisy roundabout on the road out to the new Nana Teresa International Airport. Anyone could leave the country, anyone could own a car and everyone did. Girls walked provocatively, arm-in-arm, walked straight at you, teetering around the gaps in the uneven pavements on high heels, expecting any man to get out of their way. Glued to their phones, they swayed across the packed streets, ignoring the hooting cars, from shop window to shop window. Sokoli felt better and more confident as they stood aside at the approach of this old man with his big moustache and old overcoat and walking stick, but he was little gratified by this implicit sign of respect, for to him, a relic from a different time, he expected it from any woman and anyway they all looked like prostitutes now.

Yes, he felt alone. He felt the twenty years he had spent in the mountains since the end of the regime. Although he had suffered badly after his disgrace and sacrifice, he still curiously missed the fear. The order and certainty that it had brought to things, the power he had once cherished as a policeman before he was sent to the mines. He had been an obedient servant but the master was gone. He was irrelevant now, save only for the one thing he had come to Tirana to find. The link in a chain. A link in the chain of his guilt and the means to break it.

There were huge advertising hoardings on the sides and on the tops of virtually all of the buildings. The city was now a cauldron of colour, life, activity and noise. Sokoli crossed over

Skanderbeg Square and climbed up the steps of the Opera House, ordered a Turkish coffee and sat under the high canopy in the shade, squinting into the sun, watching the seething mass of pedestrians and traffic in lawless exhaust-laden confusion as each man, woman and child took their chance on the cobbles of the Square in the moving maze of dodgems under the scream of the whistles of black-uniformed traffic cops on pedestals.

There was a time, he thought, when there had been order, when the police had been feared and obeyed. He bought a pack of cigarettes from a gypsy beggar and, for another Lek coin, a lighter with a black eagle on red.

He lit a cigarette, gazing over the noise and heat of the Square at the old mural high above the massive arcade of the National History Museum. He was surprised that they had kept the mural and had not brought it down or effaced it. Or replaced it with Western-style advertisements. But the thirteen mosaic figures were still there, the tallest 20 feet high, all proud and strong in stirring primary colours, at the centre a young woman of clear and evident virtue in traditional dress with a rifle held aloft and, inspired by high moral ideas, called out in mute vigour across the square for obedience from the seething and indifferent mass. Around her, her healthy and determined mosaic companions from the past defended their country against foreign invaders – he could see the ancient Illyrians, the mountain fighters' resistance to the Ottoman Turks led by Skanderbeg, the partisan fighters of World War Two and the communists under Enver Hoxha. The weakling puppet exile King Zog had never been included. The only change from the old days was that the red star had been removed from the flag.

A chair scraped.

"You know what to do?" A big man sat down in the chair next to him with a long sigh. "You know where it all is?" His words were followed by a long high wheeze, as if his lungs were scuffed leather bellows catching up with the effort of speaking.

Sokoli thought he recognised this man from somewhere. Probably an old Sigurimi Colonel, but he couldn't be sure because the man didn't take off his dark sunglasses. And anyway, it had been thirty-five years since Sokoli had left the secret police. Fifteen of those years had been spent in the mines. The man could be anyone.

"Yes. I don't know if anything will still be there. But I have the keys."

"Good then – we will wait till dusk and then go in with you so you won't be disturbed. We have to trust you to know where to look. Everyone else who worked on those experiments is dead. You're the only one left." The ends of his full lips creased upwards in a half smile. "It was difficult to find you up there in the mountains. But the house in the Block is being demolished. So you have to do it now."

"I do not want you in there with me." Sokoli knew this was harsh, even if the man had been a subordinate, and tried to soften the reprimand, "It's a private matter for me. The Quiet Room. I want you to stay outside."

Aware that the man was sweating under his dark clothes, Sokoli wanted to talk, to thank him, to make some contact. "We were so proud, weren't we? So proud? And so cruel? Now it's all gone."

"We'll take care of you, Sokoli. You can trust us. Just take what you find to the lawyer."

The man got up slowly from his chair with another high whiny wheeze, held out his hand, thought better of it, put some coins on the table and stepped slowly between missing pavings and cracks down the white Opera House steps into the crowd. He didn't look back.

Sokoli watched him go. The midday call to prayer came out with a harsh crackle over the speakers of the old mosque across the road, the mournful sound curling out from the minaret in the dust and the dead heat of the sun. Under his breath, Sokoli prayed to Allah that he would find what he was seeking. He held his hand up to his mouth as he muttered the words of his prayer – he was still not accustomed to being free to pray.

Part One

Zana

1

London

The offices of Hobbs, Tench, Christey took up several of the upper floors of an elegant building in Soho Square, overlooking a small green and leafy park with a white wooden-beamed shelter in the middle. It was a prestigious address, befitting one of the most successful new advertising agencies. In the park outside, lunch-timers sat in the mild sunshine, protected in an island of calm against the background murmur of the thick traffic and the rampant retail trade in Oxford Street, just a block away.

Zana Sokoli sat in her own office on the Campaign Planners floor, her desk piled high with client information – statistics, brochures, details of competitors, looking at the artwork and copy for the newest campaign. Behind her on the wall, she had hung framed prints of her favourite advertisements. Fred Spear's *"Enlist"* took pride of place in the centre, the simple single word appearing in big letters on the bottom right of a picture of a woman, holding her tiny baby close in her arms, falling between dark rocks at the bottom of the Atlantic after the *Lusitania* was torpedoed by a German U-boat in 1915.

A senior copywriter and a middle-ranking Art Director were slumped in their seats opposite her, one an Englishman of Pakistani extraction and the other a Chinese from Hong Kong, both wearing nearly identical outfits of t-shirts, jeans and trainers. Both had shaved their heads so as to disguise encroaching baldness and both were looking bad-tempered at her reaction to the result of their creative efforts which stood on an easel behind them.

"The market is saturated with birth control devices. It's got to be more clear, relevant, simple, decent. Dirty jokes and anything humorous will back-fire. I'm sure of it." Zana frowned and gazed through her glasses past their heads at the back of the room, "This new chemical acts on sperm and kills it. Women won't like it. It's deeply embedded in their, I mean our, psychology. Dead sperm will only put women off. It'll defeat the purpose…so many bad connotations."

"It's a difficult subject," murmured the Pakistani, "Frankly I can't see why anyone would use it."

"Or buy it." The Chinese shrugged, "We just can't get an angle on this."

She studied a picture on the far wall - a big 1879 poster for the Diebold Safe and Lock Company showed a frustrated Satan and his other devil safe-crackers, red, be-horned, naked, cloven-footed and hairy, sitting in despair amongst discarded crow-bars and other implements in a fiery hell around an unbroken Diebold steel safe. She was making as much progress as Satan was and was just as frustrated. "Frankly, I don't think it will appeal to men either, actually, it seems to defeat the whole purpose, danger and delight of having sex. The risk factor."

"Yeah, but that's the whole point isn't it? You're female. You would see it like that. You want live sperm, but you don't want the risk. So how do we crack it? How do we make that attractive to men? We don't want to look like pre-coital undertakers, do we?"

Zana sucked her teeth. "It's psychological for both men and women. I mean what is the practical difference between stopping live sperm in its tracks with rubber or an IUD and delivering dead sperms?" Zana took a deep breath and tapped her pencil on the desk, "So, if we can identify that difference, we'll have it. In other words, what is the unique selling point?" She put her hands on her head and leant back in her chair,

"It's fail-safe. That's all we've got to work on. I want you to go away and read, ask questions, visit the factory, talk to the client then sit down and attack the problem again. Then drop it and do something else and let your sub-conscious mind work and wait for the Eureka moment."

The two men had heard it before. It wasn't helping them.

"Please go back, start again and come up with three new ideas and artwork for something that is fail-safe, but don't tell how it works. Nobody's interested in death…..spin it, make it positive, give it life, choice, freedom from….," She waved her arms, "You know. Give it density of content, elegance of form."

"Like you, Zana." The Pakistani smirked and the two men took down their efforts from the easel and shambled out morosely. Zana heard their voices as they went down the corridor and stopped at the water-cooler. She could hear the loud remark of the Pakistani, probably the more imaginative of the two. "She's just a sworn virgin from the Strait of Otranto."

"What's that?" She heard the Chinese cough as he took a swig of water.

"It's what Albanian women do when their men have gone – you know, blood-feuds etc.

They become sworn virgins and dress up as men and take the reins. Like Marka Dushku, the boss at Pharcutrix."

"Mmm. Pity," said the Chinese. "She's beautiful, though. What a waste." He considered. "Could we use that idea? You know, something like no need for sworn virgins with this wonderful new dead-cert secret contraceptive?"

"Dunno. If we can't come up with something we'll be out and she'll be out."

Zana heard them throw their plastic cups into the bin and disappear down the length of the corridor. She knew, of course, that Pharcutrix Chemicals was the client for the contraceptive campaign, but she had never met Marka Dushku. She would have to do a little bit of research on that one. But not now. She was hungry. It was lunch time. As she took up her coat, the 'phone rang. It was some girl from Account Management and she told Zana that there seemed to be a new punter wanting to discuss a new campaign.

"But that's a new account - your department, not mine!" Zana's eyes wandered to a poster on the wall for an Ivor Novello musical from the Second World War.

"But he asked for you. Personally by name, Zana, I don't know why. Could you just speak to him, please? See if you can reel him in. If so, we'll take it up from there."

"What's his name?" There was a click on the line as the girl put through the outside call without any more introduction.

"Miss Sokoli? Zana Sokoli?" The male voice was warm, calm, confident. A little bit plummy. The enunciation was too considered and meticulous for anyone under 70 or thereabouts, "My name is Audley Barty. I'm calling you from the London Institute of Occult Research."

She liked his voice, "Well, that makes a change from cars, soap, handbags, hair-colour, perfume and baked-beans, Mr. Barty." She edited out the thought of the latest project, which she found distasteful, had been foisted upon her and which she knew was doomed to failure.

He laughed. "I'd like you to come over and see what we do. The Board of Trustees have decided we need to start advertising. A break with tradition, you could say, after only about one hundred years of dignified reserve."

She thought it sounded pretty straightforward. A small account for a niche service product in a market populated by the already credulous. It wasn't going to bring in large fees or change anybody's life.

"I'd be interested to take a look, Mr. Barty." If she was thrown out on the contraceptive, she might be able to get back in on the back of happy mediums and spiritual trances.

"You could attend one or two of our courses, get a real feel for what we do and how we try to help people." Audley Barty's tone of voice had a kind warmth under his slightly clipped speech, "Lonely people, grieving people, help us reach out, as they say. Would you have time?"

Without warning, she saw herself clearly, from a distance, as if she was standing at the other end of the room, looking at herself at her desk. His comment had touched her. It was as if he held a door open, inviting her to step through. Zana saw herself at the desk, the telephone receiver held to her ear under her dark mane of hair, the beginnings of a frown, disquiet in her hazel-coloured eyes behind her spectacles. It was as if, unlike the devil on the wall, he had managed with two simple phrases to break into her reserve, had cracked the safe and opened it and in it she saw her loneliness, geekiness - work obsessed, isolated, without any real family, empty. Why had those two phrases cut through her without warning? *Lonely people, grieving people.*"

She checked the wobble in her voice. "I am freelance, Mr. Barty. So I'm sure I can make time for you."

The appointment made, Zana put the 'phone down. She decided not to have lunch. She walked over to the window and watched the people down below in the square, slipping back into her dream life, pretending that she was standing on a grand balcony about to give a rousing speech to her faithful subjects as they milled about beneath her feet. After all, she really didn't belong here. Or anywhere, if she was honest. She deserved a palace, a prince, a ballroom, white marble terraces with tinkling fountains, at least two horse-drawn carriages and a disconcerting array of great wardrobes with infinite choices of dresses and shoes.

How had she come to be a work-for-hire dogsbody in the miserable and pointless world of persuading people that they needed things they didn't? And pretending to know about sex when she had never had a lover in her 29 years.

Because Zana was, after all, the granddaughter of a great king. She was a princess in hiding. And she was a princess waiting.

2

"Once upon a time there was a great king," her grandmother had always started her story with these same words, "He was called the White King of the Eagles and he lived in a small kingdom by the warm sea, and the kingdom was full of mountains and fierce warriors, strong and handsome, who were faithful to him and had kept all the marauding foreigners from the borders to keep them and their wives and sons and daughters safe and well. The women were beautiful and adored their menfolk. In winter the snows fell and in spring the clear waters gushed down the mountains to the rich plains which were full of good things to eat. The summer harvests were plentiful and everyone was happy."

As time passed, Zana had begun to forget her mother. The fissure of the shock when she was so young, dragged from her sleep by soldiers and taken through the mountains in the night had sunk below her consciousness, and the bed-time stories told by her grandmother had replaced the memories of pain and confusion. The strange journey, the strange cities, an old woman she had not recognised, the long train journey across Europe. The cold ferry journey across a grey sea and the big white cliffs of a country where Zana could not understand a word of the strange language spoken by these people with their pallor and white skin and pale eyes and hair. This was the age of something she knew now to have been the punk rebellion, general decay, lots of strikes and resentment and anger. The people in this country seemed to be in many tribes who disliked each other. Each town and village had people from at least two of the tribes, living together in the same place, not like in the mountain villages where she came from. You could tell them by their clothes and, when her ear became better attuned, by their accents. Zana was very confused about it. From what she could tell, they didn't actually kill each other, like the men did in the mountains. It was all words and tension and understated behaviour played out in games to show where one was in a very subtle and complicated hierarchy.

But all this had sunk under the coverlet of a life with her grandmother who had almost smothered her in a warm mantle of security in the big private house with its statues, fish pond and green lawns in a place called Sussex. The frightening people with leather jackets, spiky dyed hair, chains and torn jeans and bits of metal through their noses all seemed to belong in the town where Zana went to be fitted with her first school uniform. There were none in the Sussex village where she had arrived and stopped. Zana could still remember the scratchy grey wool skirt and the blazer which was much too big and let in the September air, so she never felt warm for the whole of her first term at the village school.

But there were times when the collar of the mantle was turned down by a cold gust of memory and Zana could recall things with chilly remembrance, although with time this faded.

"There were poets who told of grand battles and magic stories of beautiful spirits who would live in the mountain streams and be summoned by songs of the women. The spirits were called the *Zana* and that is where you come from….so you are very special… "

When Zana had arrived at the school on the village green she found that she was not welcome. The other children heard her strange accent, sensed her foreignness and ignored her. They mocked her dark eyebrows, crooked teeth and her glasses. She lived in the big house above the village, which made Zana even more remote for them. When her grandmother had made an effort and invited two of the other girls to tea at the big house, the other two had played together by the pond and had virtually evaded Zana. After they left, Zana had learnt that one, Molly Travis, who had been trying to kill the carp in the pond with a stick and some stones from the gravel drive, had been sick because Grandma's foreign cuisine had upset her stomach.

Things got worse when Zana was prescribed a brace on her teeth to make them more straight. On Sundays, which Zana would dread all the way through each preceding week, Grandma Zana would dress up in her normal clothes, but would then each Sabbath put on a calf-length coat of wool-felt which was heavily embroidered in black and white and red patterns and motifs and had bulging outer sleeves with rows of shiny metal pins with stones set in them. She would pile her hair up on top of her head and sit in the front pew with Zana in her school uniform and the rest of the congregation would instinctively sit behind them, leaving the two alone on the front pew. Grandma Zana did not seem to notice the amusement of the teenagers in the congregation at her hairstyle and the silly gestures they made behind her back. She would leave Zana isolated in solitary and acute embarrassment and emerge later from the confession box, bent over, crumpled and in tears. The priest would emerge from the box looking rather stunned and shame-faced while the rest of the faithful flock turned their eyes down as they filed out.

From then on, Zana spent most of the time without saying a word unless it was strictly required in lessons. She hated opening her mouth at all, knowing that it would show her teeth-brace with its ghastly shiny metal and pink plastic inserts. Sick of being called *Dracula* in the playground, she found a way of shortening the playground hours by sitting on a drain cover hidden in a small gorse spinney between the school building and the heath, entertaining herself with her dreams. It was her secret place, in summer a golden-yellow flowered dome with the dense scent of honey, and in winter just warm enough (if she put on two jumpers and the dark-grey woollen leggings approved by the school), with a soft bed of dried-out gorse needles. She collected mud left by horses' hooves and built mud mountains and a castle and populated this tiny landscape with figures made of clay and paper and straw and glue and some water-colour paint which she had taken from the art-room. There were horses and pigs and a white King and six sisters and the Queen. And there was a little clay figure of Zana who she would move about amongst the imaginary peasants flocking in the fields (imaginary because she could see them and didn't need to make them and anyway, when she had tried, the dried mud bodies would flake and crumble and their heads would drop off). She would move the clay Princess Zana around from one group of peasants to another, having conversations with them about their families, womens' squabbles, their problems with the harvest and the trials of unforeseen illnesses. Everywhere she went in the mud landscape, every time she bestowed a kindness or gave advice, the people loved her and were grateful for her help. It gave her a warm glow which she would carry back into the ordinariness of the afternoon lessons.

"The King had six sisters and three were ugly and three were beautiful. They loved dressing up in the finest clothes and every afternoon they would spend an hour with their brother when they would talk about lovely things like art and music and good food. Then the Queen would come down to join them. Her name was Queen Geraldine and she was also delicate and beautiful, like a fuchsia…"

Zana never bothered to ask what a fuchsia was, it would have interrupted Grandma Zana's story, but she knew it was something very pretty.

"But the King was not happy because there arrived a nasty man who believed that the King had stolen the title and had started off as a mere tribal chieftain. We know that the King was good and had been elected to the throne by all of the people who were happy, but the nasty man was cruel and said that the White King had no right to reign over the kingdom and didn't believe in kings and thought that the peasants should rule the land. The peasants who toiled in the fields were beguiled by this nasty man who tricked them and said that if they got rid of the King then he would look after them all much better and they would all share in the harvest and the fishes from the sea and the gold and silver from the mountain caverns and rivers and everything else, so the peasants took down their hunting rifles and marched to the palace."

Zana had never taken to Mr. Wilson, the head primary teacher. He had something about him that dredged her memory and brought back little sharp-edged stones of discomfort. She was scared of him, didn't trust him. He had authority and enjoyed it. He wasn't at all like Alban the gardener, who was nice.

"The people all observed the ancient laws which had been written down by a wise man long, long ago. It said that you must trust one another and not do any harm and everything would be good. But if you stole something, or killed someone, or ran off with somebody else's wife then the family of the owner or of the dead man or of the husband would be entitled to kill you and this was called a blood-feud. Many people died and the blood-feuds would be stacked up for generations in a big pile of tit-for-tat. But the rule was that nobody could kill anyone inside their own house, so sometimes men would live for years without going out at all. And the women would bring them food and drink and look after them."

Zana did not like this part. She liked the next part better.

"The King tried to stop all this. He tried to change the old laws. He stood on the balcony of the palace, proud and handsome and tall in his white uniform with gold epaulettes and many medals which shone in the sun, and waved to the crowds. But the nasty man stood up on a soap-box and had a trumpet loud-speaker and interrupted him with his rude voice and, with the beguiling tones of the devil, he turned the peasants' minds against the King."

"But then two mountain spirits appeared and began to sing. Their names were Zana," Her grandmother would always stop her story at this point and kiss her and stroke her hair, "and Dora."

"Dora was so very, very pretty and Zana was not so pretty but much more resourceful and much braver. Together they sang a magic song which was so beautiful that it made the peasants cry and love their King again, and men who heard it lost their wish to kill each other."

The warm glow became stronger when Zana was 13 and she could imagine that the White King loved her too, that he could see her real beauty behind her dark eyebrows, crooked teeth and her glasses, so cruelly mocked by her classmates. She began to create a certainty that Alban the gardener loved her and that he was secretly a prince in disguise and that Mr. Wilson was the nasty man who also secretly loved her and hoped that Zana would be able to make him nice again. She could conjure them in her mind – Alban visualised in a prince's uniform and Mr. Wilson in a dark cloak, both frustrated in their quest for her love, both obsessed by it, ready to fight each other for her approval. She started to embellish the stories with this conflict, reaching a point when both men were infused by their wanting her love, and then they would in her mind suddenly step out of the tiny landscape and become full-sized and then she would part her legs under the grey wool skirt, rub herself, gently caressing herself in front of them while the men looked on, gasping with excitement. They were both in her power, Mr. Wilson enfeebled. It was the most comforting thing Zana could imagine. She would wait until her own breathlessness subsided and then would carry the heat of the warm glow back to class, where she was able to absorb the lessons from Mr. Wilson with calm and cool equanimity – almost indifference.

"The King was so grateful to Zana that he fell in love with her and she had a beautiful baby girl. The Queen and the six sisters were happy about it too. The little baby girl grew up in the mountains and she too met a handsome officer and had a baby girl called Zana. And that is you, my dear. So you are the secret grand-daughter of a King and that is why I sent some men to get you…."

The story always ended there. Her grandmother would stop speaking and "go into herself" for a few minutes. It was only after she had heard the ending of the story many, many times that Zana began to understand that there was something else at work in her grandmother's mind when she reached this point in the story, like another ending but much more sad, which she didn't want Zana to know about. It seemed to pass quickly and Zana was always happy when it did because she loved her grandmother and didn't like to see her in pain.

3

Zana heard voices and turned away from the window. Lunchtime was over and the employees were getting back to their desks down the corridor. Her recollections disturbed, she went over to sit at her desk, yawning, listless, waiting for her memories to subside before she could concentrate on the afternoon work at Hobbs, Tench, Christey.

She yawned again. In the intake of breath and then the outbreath, she was struck by the two notes she had made. She recognised them. They were the beginning of the softest of songs which her grandmother had sung to her, made her learn, over and over again. The *Soft Songs* her grandmother Zana had called them. She began to repeat them again under her breath, her mindfulness of the present vanishing under a rush of reminiscence.

One day, Zana had been in the spinney and the soft rush of the breeze in the gorse and the mellow warmth of her swelling dreams was broken by a snapping twig. Three boys had discovered her secret kingdom and, while she watched, proceeded to stamp all over it, kicking her dreams to pieces, the dried mud and straw flying all over the place, the white king crushed. Tears streaming down her face, she went for the biggest one with a tenacious venom, strengthened by full justification, screaming breathlessly as she tore at his ears and bit into his nose and face. The other two ran off and soon Mr. Wilson appeared. There was pandemonium in the playground, the boy was rushed to hospital and Zana was reprimanded and Grandmother was forced to apologise to the boy's parents. It came to light afterwards that Molly Travis had told the boys what to do and they had followed her orders in return for a peek into her knickers. It was Zana's second introduction to the betrayal and unfairness of real life and the realisation that she could not carry on living in her dream world for much longer.

When Grandmother learnt from Mr. Wilson that Zana was so isolated, living in another world, and that he was worried, she listened to his recommendations.

"I am sure she is bright enough," he had said, "perhaps it would help if she had elocution lessons so that her accent would go and she would be able to fit in and make friends more easily?"

Elocution lessons were given by Mr. Wilson himself. Mr. Wilson in real life was completely different from the Mr. Wilson in her stories and Zana had followed instructions, despite her strange wariness of this man in authority, whose corrections of her accent, although patient and well-meant, reminded her of a man she remembered in a different part of her mind. A man unconnected, in a uniform, who had been with her mother and her father and then had vanished and left, well before she was wrenched from her bed in the dead of night. She thought this man in the uniform might have been the nasty man in grandmother's fairy story.

Then a visit to the dentist in Lewes produced a miracle. The brace came off her teeth at last and she felt more confident. She would spend a few minutes in front of the mirror each morning, practising her smile and marvelling at the new evenness of her white teeth. At first, for a few days, she took every opportunity to smile in class. But nobody noticed and nothing changed. Her nickname *Dracula* had stuck to her. So then she forgot to smile and never laughed. But the elocution lessons became much easier.

It was then that her Grandma had patiently insisted that she learnt the Soft Songs. "These songs will protect you one day," her Grandma had told her, "when the time comes." She sounded so certain that the time would come that Zana had never asked why or what was in store or when the time would arrive. When her grandmother sang the soft songs, Zana could go straight back in her mind to her mother singing her to sleep, warm, soft and gentle. She could be with her mother again, it was so real she could feel her mother's breath, her smell of delicate fruit, her kindness in the tough closed world of the village outside. To keep this memory intact and her mother near, she did her very best to learn the soft notes, murmured and breathed them, kept her Grandma pleased, until just before her fourteenth birthday her Grandma was at last satisfied that Zana had the breathing and the tones perfect and had bought her a special sponge cake with a cream filling and strawberries on top. There was another cake for her birthday.

Zana could take herself back anytime, but she could never see her father or hear her father's voice. His presence in her memory was shrouded, a distant benevolence, always there but silent, like the stone walls of the house they lived in, providing a strong wall of safety.

When Zana was 15 years old, she had a cut-glass English accent and won a prize for standing up and reciting the poem "Grasshopper Green" (which, according to Mr. Wilson, included all sample vowels and consonants) in the village hall. She could still recite it word for word.

Grasshopper Green is a comical chap;
*   He lives on the best of fare.*
Bright little trousers, jacket, and cap,
*   These are his summer wear.*
Out in the meadow he loves to go,
*   Playing away in the sun;*
It's hopperty, skipperty, high and low,
*   Summer's the time for fun.*

Grasshopper Green has a quaint little house;
*   It's under the hedge so gay.*
Grandmother Spider, as still as a mouse,
*   Watches him over the way.*
Gladly he's calling the children, I know,
*   Out in the beautiful sun;*
It's hopperty, skipperty, high and low,
*   Summer's the time for fun.*

By the time Zana was 16, she had won a scholarship to a girls boarding school and moved away, seeing her grandmother only in the holidays.

At 18 she went up to Oxford to read psychology, literature and languages. Her heroine was Eve Kosofsky Sedgwick (particularly, *Jane*

Austen and the Masturbating Girl) which, despite the arcane academic language which she thought beat about the bush too much, really spoke to her sense of isolation and at 24, her thesis for her doctorate, based on Sedgwick's work, was entitled *The Male, Nationalism, Legends and Motherhood in Albanian Culture*, a well-researched dissertation on the foundations and dominant sub-conscious links in the male psychology to mothers and the way in which this translated into nationalistic identification with conflict-driven male heroes, attachment and motivation as group protectors of the mother-country as a mother-figure, fuelled by legend, music and other cultural stimuli. It pointed out that this phenomenon was recognisable in many different areas of human tribal activity, such as jingoism, war, and watered–down areas such as football mania and team sport supporters. The thesis drew on Sedgwick's ideas that male tribal bonding required a female object, a fantasy figure, a trophy whose conquest indicated prowess over the rest of the tribe. It concluded by pondering why the original source of the love of the mother for her sons could be so translated (or distorted) into an activity which threatened all mothers and all young girls as potential mothers.

Her thesis was well received and, to her surprise, won an award. But she had gained a reputation among her fellow doctorate students for being very serious, self-contained and really not much fun to be with.

Then, when she came down from Oxford and got her first job in advertising, her grandmother had told her the other story.

4

It was obvious to Zana that her grandmother was losing her memory. She was distant, forgetful, petulant and depressed. The big house in the Sussex village had grown in on itself, Alban had left to get married to a girl in Mayfield, the pond was full of stagnant weed. The interior was neglected and dirty and paint was peeling off the windows and sills. The local doctor insisted that Grandma Zana could no longer cope and was in imminent danger of hurting herself if she was left alone. Zana had spoken to him about arranging a local carer in the interim and selling the house and putting old Zana in a nice retirement home which specialised in the care of the elderly with encroaching dementia. She contacted her grandmother's solicitor in Lewes who promised to sort it out with the trustees of old Zana's estate. She had, of course, read about the history of Albania, but she was desperate to hear the truth from the old lady who had had the courage to organise her escape across the border during the Cold War and had saved her from a life under the Communist dictator. Zana wanted to coax the reality from her grandmother before it

47

disappeared under the clouds of dementia with her memory cells

As a special treat for old Zana's birthday, Zana drove down to Sussex in her rusty Citroën deux-chevaux and then took her grandmother to Glyndebourne for a performance of Igor Stravinsky's opera, *The Rake's Progress*. She was shocked at the price of the tickets and could barely afford them, but went ahead anyway. They had lunch on the lawns, sitting by the banks of the pond, the old lady in a canvas folding seat and Zana on a rug, producing salmon sandwiches, a prepared salad and lemonade from a hamper. The old house and the newly-built auditorium kept the wind at bay and the clean green smell of freshly-mown grass saturated the air from parallel lines of dark green and shining emerald down to the trees at the edge of the pond, whose surface was ruffled by the slight wind and the mouths of the fish which languidly broke the surface. The scene, lit by warm and soporific sunshine, the tree shadows stretching imperceptibly towards them across the lawns, was an idealised scene, the essence of the land which had given them a home.

Fortified by the hamper, her grandmother pulled her shawl around her and began speaking with a trace of urgency, her tone surprisingly precise. "It's time to stop the fairy stories, Zana. You are old enough. You have grown up now."

Zana felt very, very sad. The stories had been her support, after all. She let the silence flow over them, listening to the distant murmur of other opera-goers pick-nicking in the distance, the occasional pop of champagne corks and trills of laughter. She let her grandmother speak without interrupting her.

"Your mother was my daughter and the daughter of King Zog. He was a tremendous flirt and a very charming man. Out of us two, my sister Dora was the more beautiful and had a much better singing voice. I was more plain, more work-a-day..." Grandma was rattling along, trying to get through her story as fast as possible, maybe worried that her memory would go before she got to the end, "When Dora refused Zog's advances, he turned to me, he was kind and generous at first and I was young and naïve and I fell in love with him, believing in him. It was not returned, really, at all. I became his peccadillo, a little game" She glanced at Zana from her seat, her hands tightly gripping the arms of her chair, "Love was unknown. The Albanian language had no word for "love" or "to love". I was sent out of the way back to the mountains and gave birth to your mother back in the village nunnery."

"King Zog was deposed and went into exile in 1939." Grandma Zana slowly took another, larger, sip of lemonade and smiled. "Dora went with him and had asked Zog to take me too as her, well, handmaiden I suppose – little more. By this time he had lost interest in me and was after Dora, so he agreed." She studied some people in evening dress who were playing frisbie under a willow, "We thought we would be away for a few weeks. But we never went back and," tears formed under her lashes and she looked down at her feet, swallowed some more lemonade, "so I lost my daughter."

A clench of grief stopped her speaking. She tried to start again, but an undercurrent wave of another memory came and silenced her before she could resume. Zana sensed that it was this one, the deep unspoken memory, which held her grandma's pain. She waited.

"Zog left England. Dora and I lived together for a long time, until the late 60s, but then Dora was invited back to Albania by the Communists and, to my shock and disbelief, she accepted. She had done the wartime seaside concert circuit in England and it had come to nothing. She was easily enticed back to Albania by promises of becoming a national emblem of the new State." Grandma Zana smiled and looked across the lawns with an expression of deep loss and remorse. "We never saw each other or spoke again."

Zana let the moment lengthen until her grandmother's emotion had softened.

"You loved him, didn't you, King Zog, very much?"

Her grandmother hesitated, "Yes." Her face softened, "I was young."

So that was it, thought Zana. The pain of love gone sour with the King's indifference, the illegitimate child unacknowledged and then abandoned and then….She waited until the scar of grief had passed and her grandmother's familiar resolve crept back into her face, "My father?"

"Your father was just a village boy made good."

"What happened to my mother?"

There was a long pause as her grandmother considered the willows in the distance and, when she replied, she was clipped and final. "Zana, I am afraid that she died. Your father betrayed her."

Her Grandma looked into the distance. Across the lawn a plump man with white hair and linen suit and a panama hat was making his way towards the pair of them on the grass. Grandma Zana seemed to shake her head as she shifted in her chair so that she had turned her back to him. As the man stopped and turned away, she suddenly reached over and gripped Zana's hand. "Never forget, my own darling. Never forget the Soft Songs." She gripped and pumped Zana's hand, "They will protect you from the scars of passion, from sentiment, from the pain of love and betrayal...."

The curtain bell rang from the house.

"...when the time comes."

The words hung in their mutual silence as they packed their things and went in to their seats.

5

The Rake's Progress was a disappointment and Zana regretted not having checked the story and libretto before she had bought the tickets. Sitting next to her grandmother in the cloying warmth of the packed auditorium, she became aware that old Zana was restless and not really paying attention or enjoying the music, the singing or the story. The set design by David Hockney was, despite having been first produced in 1975, too modern for her to put into context.

Zana, too, could not concentrate on the story. She was thinking about what old Zana had said. The opera's simple moral tale of Tom Rakewell and Anne Trulove and Tom's weakness of character and decline into madness at the hands of the devil, Nick Shadow, seemed pale beside her own story. Mother Goose's brothel, Baba the Turk, the famous bearded lady, the "fantastic Baroque Machine" turning stones into bread, all seemed quite silly and pointless. Her grandmother was fast asleep during the interval and stayed asleep, her slight snore too gentle to be heard by anyone else in their row.

They drove back to the house in silence. Zana put her grandma to bed and stayed up looking at the overgrown garden in the moonlight. She thought about her parents and their tragedy. Why had her father done that terrible thing to her mother? It stayed in her mind until she went to sleep.

She dreamed about Tom Rakewell. Her mother appeared, face shadowed, as Ann Trulove. They were dancing around a fantastic baroque machine which became a black and red street barrel organ with brass pipes, played by an organ-grinder who was a woman with a beard in a man's evening suit and top hat. As the woman turned the crank, she grinned at Zana and the sound of the barrel organ became a woman's voice, soft and warm. Nick Shadow came through a hole in the ground and Zana heard the voice of her mother who had sung her to sleep when she was eight. Nick Shadow was dressed in the uniform of the secret police and held a crow-bar which he raised above his head. The plump man with white hair and linen suit and a panama hat came through a red curtain and struggled with Nick Shadow, but Nick Shadow changed into someone else, a shadow of a man whose strength was felt rather than seen, who broke free and raised the crow-bar above his head and brought it down on the barrel organ and it broke, but the bearded lady kept turning the crank and all Zana could hear were abrasive, rasping sobs. She woke up crying.

The doctor and the carer came in the morning. Arrangements had been made. Grandma would go to a home in the Isle of Wight, the house sold and the contents either auctioned or put in storage.

Zana spent two days up in the attic, going through the old packing cases and trunks and sorting things out. What she was really looking for were clues.

6

London

Zana liked the atmosphere inside the Institute of Occult Research. A high entrance portico with white pillars covered four stone steps up to the black front door which led to a long cool tiled hallway with the reception and the library off it. Downstairs was a canteen and upstairs were the meeting rooms. She had once been to Kyoto on a university trip to Japan and the inside of this building, once the door was closed and despite being in a side street in Bloomsbury, London, managed to have the same damask, dense, dreamy atmosphere of meditation.

Audley Barty was in the President's room on the first floor and rose from his desk, or almost jumped to his feet, when she was shown in.

She accepted the offer of tea and when the receptionist had left, Audley Barty looked at her for what seemed to Zana a long time before he spoke.

"Well, welcome Miss Sokoli." He didn't say it, but she could hear the silent "at last".

"Zana, please." She had liked him immediately.

"Then please call me Audley." She had done some research on him in the agency's archives and now she had finally met him she could see that Audley Barty lived up to his reputation. He had a shock of lengthy thick white hair and wore a cream linen suit with braces which seemed to her a trifle redundant over his white-striped blue shirt and bulky girth. The matching pink bow-tie and breast-pocket handkerchief completed a picture of one of those flamboyant men who had lived life – and still lived life - at full tilt, as he was, without apology. According to the research she had read, Audley was full of energy, always curious, interested in everything. Along with his extensive publishing empire, he had branched out into internet subscription television and other media-oriented activities and ran his empire from a smart office in Mayfair, assisted by his lioness p.a called Twilda Tonlinson. Zana had done a search on his group of companies and knew that the last-year's consolidated accounts for his group showed many millions of pounds in profit, but his declared primary interest (according to *Who's Who?*) was in the occult and his presidency of the Institute.

While Audley talked about the Institute and promised to show her the library, Zana scanned the books and papers on his desk. There were piles of handwritten notes, a bound first edition of the poems of Aleister Crowley and a thumbed copy of what looked like an unpublished thesis entitled, as Zana could easily read upside-down, *The Male, Nationalism, Legends and Motherhood in Albanian Culture (2005).*

He saw her recognise the title of her own university treatise. "A very interesting piece of work. You have my congratulations…"

Zana thanked him cordially, wondering what else about her he had bothered to find out. But he went on. "I want you to get a thorough understanding of the Institute, before you start," Audley was saying, "I'll keep you under my wing," He paused and laughed, "that is of course if you want to do it?"

Zana said she would be delighted, that it was presumably an easily-definable market and that the Institute had an obvious uniqueness in its selling point – it was the only occult research establishment in the country, after all. She would be willing to start right away.

"We want to broaden our base, expand and become more main-stream. More populist."

She would think about it and come up with some ideas. Could she look at the brochure which outlined the courses on offer?

He handed a brochure to her as they went down to the library. It was a high-ceilinged room with aging oak bookshelves full of faded and arcane leather bound and tooled volumes. A studious-looking girl sat in the corner at a reading desk. "You shall have free reign, Zana," Audley whispered enthusiastically, "but please don't remove those volumes over there from the building. They are irreplaceable." He pointed to three lines of shelves which had locked glass doors.

"Now, let me show you the courses." He opened the brochure, put it down on a table and took out a pair of rimless glasses from an inside pocket. "Naturally, all of these are up-dated on our web-site."

He turned each of the pages slowly, waiting for her reaction to his suggestions before he turned the next. "Mediumship? Tarot? Fortune-telling? Past-Life?"

"Actually, Audley, I *am* a little bit more interested in the past as well as the future. You know, connections…"

"That's unusual. I mean for one so young." He turned the last page, "Here's one which might be interesting for you." He held the brochure and showed her. "It's a new one which we haven't tried before…"

Zana read the item entry – *Anna Bullock, Ancestral Guidance*. "That sounds interesting, certainly." She murmured.

"If you like the look of it, I'll have it booked it for you my dear."

"OK, thanks, I'll look forward to it."

He showed her to the door and opened it for her. "One little thing though," Audley said, holding the door open, "You will probably encounter my nephew at that course, if he shows up. To be frank, I try to help him, but he's a little bit of a black sheep. *Le mouton noir de la famille.* You might find him a little strange. He's called Lionel, Lionel Barty. Best give him a wide berth and steer clear to windward if you can."

As she went down the front steps to the street and he closed the door, she saw his round face smiling down at her. He had an expression of glee, as if he was a little boy who had just been given a present which he had longed for.

7

"The client wants to see you." Her boss's voice, normally friendly, had been curt and to the point, "At their office. Alone."

"What about the creative boys? The Account Manager?"

"They've seen the boys. It was no good. They don't want to see anyone else. They want to see you by yourself. Ask for Mark Dushku, the CEO."

This could only mean one thing - she had lost the account for the agency. If she could just hang on to Audley's Institute account, then she might be able to stay in her job. Also, as she had to admit to herself, it was quite a relief - she knew that she couldn't do anything with the dead sperm chemical contraceptive.

She put on a black two-piece and high-heels, put her hair up in a pony-tail and took a taxi over Waterloo Bridge to the south of the river and then along the bank eastward to the new developments around the Oxo Tower, where she found Pharcutrix Chemicals in an anonymous steel and glass building. Resigned and fatalistic, anxious to get it over with, she was received in reception and shown up in the lift to the top floor where an office with full-length glass gave a view out over the river below. In it, back to her, sat a bulky individual in a dark suit with short dyed black hair. When the figure swivelled the chair round to face her, Zana was shocked to see that it was a woman, dressed in the style of a man's suit. Of course, she could have foreseen this - Dushku was an Albanian name. The woman had obviously changed her forename from Marka to Mark.

Marka Dushku was about 55 years of age, plump and maternal-looking and Zana sensed an underlying warmth which managed to transfuse the steel sieve of her apparent objectivity, business-like approach and her attempt at manliness. She struck Zana as the kind of woman who had been forced to look at the world through a fencing-mask, one step removed, a little bit of an oddity like the bearded lady in *The Rake's Progress*. Zana sensed that Marka was a woman who had been forced to live in a man's world, to become hard-headed and take the reins. She had relinquished her femininity completely. Zana instinctively knew that deaths of her men had made her like that, that she was a Sworn Virgin, a fighter for survival in a man's world. Zana liked her as much as she liked Audley.

They talked at length. By the time the interview was over Zana had had (1) an acknowledgement that the dead sperm idea was never going to work (2) a lecture on male redundancy in the progress of the human race (3) a full and complete breakdown of her entire life and education (4) an invitation to apply for a job as the assistant vice-president in training for the whole group which covered not just pharmaceuticals but electronics and a whole plethora of other activities (5) to sign a very rigid confidentiality agreement, and (6) in return, a promise to receive a confidential psychological assessment of her state of mind and free counselling.

Mind reeling, unable to think straight, she tumbled down with the lift and walked out of the building in a haze of Technicolor possibilities.

When Marka had asked Zana if she had any questions, Zana had asked her for the usual stuff – accounts, corporate structures, detail on businesses and projects. But the burning question she left until last, "Why me?"

"Because you are perfect for us." Marka Dushku looked at Zana over the desk, her scrutiny not unkind, more a confirmation of a conclusion already reached, "You will understand me and you will understand our culture."

Two days later, when she was preparing her resignation from the agency, Zana noticed an article in *The Financial Times* that reported that Pharcutrix Chemicals (Head Office in Luxembourg) was under investigation by a Department of the European Commission. She shrugged. European Investigations were routine. It was just a matter of time before it was shelved and forgotten. But she deleted her draft resignation from her computer. She would leave it for the moment.

And also, she considered as she looked at the snarling devil and his cohorts on her wall as they surveyed the uncracked Diebold safe, whatever glittering career she could have, she knew she would one day have to come to terms with what her Grandma Zana had told her. If she didn't, the scar would never heal. Pharcutrix had done their research well. They recognised the need for *"a promise to receive a confidential psychological assessment of her state of mind and free counselling."*

Audley Barty had been kind to her. She decided she would try and do a good job for him. She would go to his Ancestral Guidance course at the Institute. She would plan a campaign for him.

Then she would join Pharcutrix and Marka
Dushku. Yes, she thought to herself, very neat.
She had it all planned out. She almost laughed.

Part Two

Lionel

8

London

"Oh! Thank God!" The woman came towards me and gave me a hug, "A Man!" I tried my best not to shrink or to flinch. "My name is Anna." She took a step back, still holding my hand, "You must be Lionel? Lionel Barty? Your uncle said you would come. Audley's a great man." She had an unusually strong grip for her lean frame and grey hair. "We needed a man." Her eyes were bright, kind and perceptive.

I slid my hand away from hers and stood at the door, looked quickly round the room and regretted coming. About thirteen women, most young and some less young, sat in a circle of chairs in the room on the top floor of the London Institute of Occult Research. I forced a smile and went over to the last empty chair in the corner by the open window.

The woman in the seat next to me waited for me to sit down before she muttered to me in a strong Irish accent tinged with curry, "Now where did a name like that come from, Mr. Lionel Barty?" She had curly grey hair and slightly bulbous eyes and wore black leggings and a black motorbike jacket. She grinned.

I was used to this. "My Father is called Jack Barty. My mother was German. She thought Lionel was a nice English name. It wasn't meant to be a joke." I replied automatically, a tiny bit terse, having repeated the same explanation countless times over the years. "She liked Bart's music and I can live with it."

The Irish lady looked away. The minor frisson between us would pass in a few minutes, I thought. I looked around the room. It was big, with high ceilings and Georgian sash windows and a huge marble fireplace supporting a large oil painting of Madame Helena Blavatsky in an ornate discoloured gold frame. Outside, a light rain fell on the Saturday crowds down below in the Bloomsbury street. I really wished I was back on the barge with the first beer of the day to cure my hangover.

I had been anxious about doing this since my uncle had nagged me to sign up. "It's for your own good, Lionel," His voice had barked at me over the telephone, "You need to confront your devils, not avoid them. You're too much like your father. You don't want to end up like him, really now do you?" He was about to hang up when he said, as an afterthought, "Dada, do you know how your father is? Has he moved?" He never said, "My brother" or "Jack", always "your father". I told him that I only knew that Jack was alive and that he still lived on the Isle of Wight. "Don't worry, I can always trace him if I need to." He put the phone down.

My uncle Audley was more my father to me than my real one. He was a successful publisher, had taken me in in my teens, put me through Law School. We were close. He was also the President of the London Institute of Occult Research and was always suggesting self-help courses which he thought would help me. I usually went along with it to make him shut up. Sometimes his concern for me could be stifling, but if I resented it sometimes my aversion was always short-lived. He genuinely cared about me.

Audley had taken on the presidency of the Institute with his usual gusto. He had widened the curriculum and the scope of the courses and workshops beyond the usual psychic mediums, tarot readers, fortune-tellers and what-not. As he said, it wasn't about belief. It was about investigation, enquiry and knowledge. He wanted to examine every single aspect of what was behind the dark veil before he died. "Belief is a killer," was his mantra and he would often cite the number of men, women and children who had died in religious and political wars and struggles over the centuries. He had a gentle contempt for any belief system, particularly those religions, basically all of them, which said that if you follow instructions when you live everything will get better when you die. He thought it was a con trick and frequently said it was the most effective con trick that had ever been devised by the human mind. He also would mutter that he wished he had dreamed it up himself because it would have been very good for his businesses.

This course was called "Ancestral Guidance". You couldn't gather anything more concrete from the programme brochure. I was anxious about what it could reveal under the iron lid under which I had bottled everything up since I was 14. That was 20 years ago and I had been acting perfectly well ever since. "Acting" is the operative word here. To explain, the Lionel Barty that I hoped everyone saw was a fairly good looking, confident, successful music lawyer, a partner in a West End practice with a string of clients and a good income. But the inside of Lionel Barty was a little bit different, as Uncle Audley knew very well. Diabetic, Alcoholic, Depressive. And maybe a position just past the beginning of the autistic spectrum. This had never been formally diagnosed, but my wife was convinced that I had Asperger's syndrome and had diagnosed this herself over the course of our short marriage and I had come to accept it with resignation. Actually, accept it with gratitude, since it was a shorthand way of explaining the eccentricity, the difference of perception, the knowledge that I was not entirely like normal people. I've always been drawn to eccentric people and liked them, have admired their freedom, their difference and their courage to accept themselves as they are. I always found them easy to get on with, easier than non-eccentrics whom I found to be rather tedious after about 30 minutes.

My wife was normal. She had a friend who was also normal, but whose daughter had been diagnosed as an acute aspergic. I had accompanied them on a shopping trip and, bored, had wandered off without explanation, knowing I could meet up with them at the café where they had said they would go after their interminable mullings-over of garments for sale in the shops. When I showed up in the café, my wife was annoyed and the friend had let slip a remark that my behaviour was exactly what her daughter would have done.

Within days, the postman had delivered virtually every published guide to Asperger's syndrome and the die was irretrievably cast. My wife carefully read every single one of the books and then asked me questions. I flipped through a few of them and had to agree with her conclusion. As I said before, it came as a relief to know that there was an explanation for the subtle difference which I had felt all of my conscious life. My uncle Audley, flippantly, called me "Dada" as a nickname and an acronym for Diabetic, Alcoholic, Depressive, Aspergic. And my wife had called it "unreasonable behaviour" before she took more than half my money and left me. Oh, and I now live on a barge on the Thames at Hammersmith Bridge next to another barge inhabited (but never sailed) by an Eastern-European porn-club owner called, appropriately, Dek. Oh, and the work has dried up, I have had no clients left since the traditional music recording industry virtually collapsed since the start of internet digital downloads. But maybe it's really because after I realised that there was nothing glamorous about legal work – even in the music business - I began to hate the job, despise my colleagues for charging huge sums of money for copying and pasting standard contracts, and lost interest. And so I'm broke. I hope you can see why I didn't welcome the idea of a baring of my soul to people I'd never met.

"Well. Welcome everyone. I am your therapist. No, more your guide, I think. My name is Anna." She looked around at us. "Now, who knows how this works? Has anybody done this work before?"

Silence. The expressions around the room varied between naked dread and cautious optimism to bright white toothy enthusiasm. A girl to my left who looked Polish had an expression of permanent despair, her whole face having changed its structure over the years to be set like that. It was impossible to imagine her smiling.

"Well, the answer is that nobody does know how or why it works, but it does." Anna looked slowly round the room, "Trust me. It's powerful stuff."

A young woman sat in the corner, gazing back at Anna, demure, quietly intent. She sat easily with a straight back, her floral dress bright, belted at the waist, confident. Her dark hair was clipped at the back with a hair clip and fell over her shoulders in thick curly waves. I hadn't noticed her before. Her strong eyebrows sheltered dark honeyed eyes above high curving cheekbones. Her face and posture seemed foreign, had an Eastern, almost gypsy, look, accentuated by the simple elegance of her dress. As I watched her, I had a slow feeling of unease. I looked down at the carpet, white spots forming on my retinas. Worried that I was running low on blood sugar, I carefully reached into my jacket pocket and took out a glucose tablet and put it into my mouth. I had to be careful. I had had much too much wine and spirits the night before with Dek and his girls on his barge. The fear of diabetic collapse was always there.

"Any of you who wish to try this, it's like this. I am your guide. But I don't want any long stories. You give a brief explanation to the group of why you wish for ancestral guidance and then you will ask other members of the group to represent your ancestors. You will position those members in the circle, aided by me, like figures on a chessboard. Then we will listen to those members as they channel, and they become, your ancestors." Anna paused, "And your ancestors will answer you. They will explain how you have become what you are now, how you were formed by the history of your DNA chain and by their experiences and feelings which are embedded and ingrained in you." She gave a low chuckle, "Don't worry, I won't force any of you to participate. I have done this many times and after all we all have families, don't we?"

Amid the nervous laughter, I glanced at the girl. She was looking at her hands, twisting them in her lap.

"Any questions before we start?" For a while, nobody moved or spoke. I tried to think of a question which would make me sound intelligent. But I couldn't think of anything. We would see what happened. I was ready to settle back as a comfortable spectator.

Then in the uncertain silence my girl, the one I was watching, slowly raised her hand. But she was beaten to it by a large pushy blonde in pink who was sitting in the centre of the group. Vivacious. You know the type.

"Please introduce yourself" said Anna.

The blonde introduced herself, but I can't remember her name now. I think she was called Cindy. I sat back in my chair and stretched out my legs, ready to be bored. I was feeling hungry and started to yawn. Looking back, I was stupid. I should have known the signs.

It went like this. Cindy had a problem with her emotions. She thought it had something to do with her parents' relationship, but she couldn't know because her mum and dad had died in a car crash. Something along the lines of a magazine agony-aunt column. Anyway, she duly walked to the centre of the circle of people, appointed some of them to be representatives for her mum and dad and her grandparents who accepted and walked into the middle of the circle and were positioned by the blonde with Anna's help. Then each representative faced another representative and revealed what they felt about them. Out of that came clarification of what problems Cindy the blonde had inherited. The representatives then formed a line in order of seniority, the oldest at the back, youngest at the front, linked by each of the older's arms being placed on the younger's shoulders. Cindy stood in front of the line, receiving the wisdom which had been revealed down the long line of inherited misery. It was mildly interesting. Certainly the representatives sounded authentic – as if they had become Cindy's real relatives. And Cindy seemed to understand the insights which were thrown up. The result of the interaction was that it became clear that Cindy's mother had never wanted children and had no maternal feelings at all. She blamed the father and resented her daughter for tying her down for life. Cindy had felt this instinctively but had never identified the cause.

She finished the session in tears and went back to her seat.

I decided that I wouldn't join in. It was too upsetting. I could happily keep my iron lid in place and wait through the day until I could escape. After all, if it ain't broke, don't fix it. My iron lid had served me perfectly well for 20 years and there was no need to reveal anything to these people.

My girl got to her feet and walked into the middle of the room.

"Please introduce yourself" murmured Anna.

She swallowed and cleared her throat. "My name is Zana. It is my grandmother's name." Her mouth started to tremble. She controlled it, then, "I never have been able to…." She looked up with shining wet dark eyes, "I need help." Her head bent and she looked at the floor. "I don't know what is wrong with me." Her hair clip came off and her dark hair fell around her face as she raised her hand to her mouth. "I cannot trust anyone. I need to find out why it happened."

Was it just me or had anyone else been affected? I glanced around the room at the circle of facial expressions, mainly sympathetic. It seemed to be just me, then, but I was the only male in the room. Zana's voice was exquisite. The only simile I can think of is a wine with layers of tastes and after-tastes, some deep, some light, some still, some moving, some thick and dark, some light and playful. A very slight foreign tint to the plummy modulation had come with her note of despair, combining depth and light in the same breath. Beautiful.

Quietly Anna stood and put her hands gently on Zana's shoulders. "Zana. Can you tell me a little about it?" Even speaking quietly, Anna's voice jarred. I just wanted to hear Zana again.

After a moment, Zana whispered something which I couldn't hear. Anna stood rigid beside her, looking uncertain. "Zana. Could you please say that again?"

"My father killed my mother. And I escaped."

I must say that Anna was very professional. She swallowed and took a little time to pull herself together. "So, then, please choose your representatives, Zana."

Anna stopped, as if listening for other voices. The room was completely still. The rain outside had stopped. The mumble of traffic and crowds had gone. After a few moments, Anna said, "I know that your mother is dead. But your father is still alive isn't he Zana?"

Zana nodded, "How did you….? Yes, I think so. Maybe I will try to find him when I understand."

"And your grandfather is dead? But your grandmother is still alive."

"Yes, but she has dementia. She cannot explain anything."

"Then, Zana, I want you to choose representatives for your grandfather on your mother's side and your mother and father. Remember it doesn't matter at all if the relative is alive or dead or the representative is male or female, what they look like or how old they are."

Zana looked slowly around the circle and then back again. She pointed to the Irish lady next to me.

"No, Zana, you must please ask the lady to be your representative and specify who she must represent…Say, "Please would you represent my…."

Zana walked over to the lady. In a stronger voice, she asked, "Please would you represent my grandfather?"

"Yes, dear." The Irish woman next to me stood up and walked on her stout legs into the centre space. Another woman of about 35, with brown hair and freckles, dressed all in brown in a county twin-set and pearls sort of way, accepted the role of Zana's mother and then Zana came back over to my corner.

"Will you please represent my father?"

Conquering my reluctance, trying not to look at her bum, I stood up and followed her into the middle of the room.

9

Anna helped Zana put us three into position. When they were done with us, the woman with the black leather jacket stood close next to the brown lady. I was drawn over by Zana to stand far away, right on the perimeter of the circle away from the window in the shadowed area by the fireplace. Madame Blavatsky looked down at me from the portrait. Her slightly hyperthyroid eyes stared at me. I glanced over at the Irish lady in the motorbike jacket. Her eyes, curiously, had the same bulge in them and oddly bore the same expression. She felt my look and returned my glance. Hands down by her sides, she gave me a little wave with her fingers. It had grown very quiet, the four of us in a bubble of silence.

Anna's voice was distant, "Zana, I want your grandfather to speak to your mother. Please draw them face to face, eye to eye." Zana complied. The two women faced each other.

"Speak grandfather. Look into your daughter's eyes. Look in your heart. Speak grandfather."

The motorbike woman looked into the county lady's eyes. Then she closed her own. "I am feeling that you are my child." She swallowed and her eyes opened again, bulged wet, her voice lowered, "I gave you your stubborn way. But I do not know you."

The motorbike lady stood up straight, spine lengthened, shoulders held back under the creak of the thick black leather. She put her fingers to the corner of her top lip and moved them slightly in the air, as if stroking an invisible moustache. With the tiny movement, I sensed an incense, not at all like the curry I had smelt on her breath. It was like smoke from a woodland fire of burning hazelwood deep in an autumn forest, or like a Turkish cigarette smelt through the doors of two hushed ante-rooms from a quiet smoker in a far library.

"I am the White King. But I treated you as a brigand treats a lost sheep. If I had known you…..."

"Are you sure it feels real?" Anna whispered, surprised.

The motorbike lady nodded slowly, holding Anna's gaze.

"Well then, now the mother?"

The brown county lady had altered her posture. She stood straight as a pine. "It was not you that brought me the pain."

Anna drew the White King behind the mother and took his hands and rested them on the mother's shoulders. "Zana, can you feel them?"

Zana nodded. Her shoulders were trembling. She put her palms under the thin belt of her dress.

"That's very good. Now then, Zana's father please...."

I walked over. The room seemed to shrink around us as I stood looking at Zana's mother. White spots appeared in front of my eyes and her face faded, her pupils lit up as if by an electric torch. It was dark. I sensed wood-smoke. A cold wood-panelled room in a small stone hut. I saw the mother kneeling at a bedside, looking up at me holding a book, its cloth cover soiled, reading to a girl under thick embroidered covers. Her breath white in the cold, she was whispering strongly and distinctly in a language I didn't understand, but I somehow had the meaning. I listened carefully, saying out loud the words I heard in that strange language:

"And I saw a mighty angel proclaiming in a loud voice, Who is worthy to break the seals and open the scroll? ..."

There came a wave of shock and revulsion as the words followed each other, engulfing me, each sounding out as the toll of a death bell.

"And they sang a new song: You are worthy to take the scroll and to open its seals. Then I heard every creature in heaven and on earth and under the earth and on the sea, and all that is in them, singing……"

Under the bed-clothes a small girl looked up at me. Her expression was still, watchful. In her dark eyes I saw a strange withering.

The cold went and the wooden room faded. Then it was gone. I was back in Bloomsbury. The brown woman's eyes still stared back into mine. But I stayed in the deep water of the after-wave, its cold still there. Her block-head belief. The danger she put us in. I felt panic. All our lives were at risk. I felt as if I was going to puke. My words came from another place. "Your words will kill us all."

The brown county lady eyes were reproachful, "My words give me strength. You know this. I know you love me and will not betray us also." Her voice was guttural. Her face was jerking sideways across my vision in sudden juddering movements and I had to concentrate on keeping it in front of me as it slid sideways again. I got her face in focus but it began flickering like a faulty computer-screen or celluloid film trapped in the teeth of a mechanical projector. I realised that my blood sugar had run out and I was having a hypoglycaemic attack.

"It was not your words. It was your own mother who killed you."

I remember that Anna rushed towards me. Behind her, I saw Zana. For a tiny moment, my vision stopped its manic flickering. Zana was outraged, as if I had insulted her or voiced a profanity. White-faced, she looked as if she wanted to bite me. "No!" She was shouting, "No, it's not true! That can't be true!"

A small white hole appeared in the celluloid and then flared bright orange outwards to the edges of my vision. "Oh not again." I heard my groan as I fell and passed out, gone before the crack of my head on the floor, darkness folding over me like a blanket.

10

There are diabetics and diabetics. Lots of them. Some take themselves and their condition very seriously indeed and tend to let it rule their lives. Constant worries about their diet, blood-tests taken every few hours and recorded in their special blood-sugar diary records with meticulous precision. These are probably the sensible ones, but they do tend to put on fat and be pale. And fairly miserable. Others rage against it and refuse to let it alter their activities in any way. You can guess which I am. One thing that all diabetics share, though, is that when they have low blood sugar they talk gibberish because the brain is being starved of the glucose which it needs to function. It's dangerous because the resulting behaviour is very close to being paralytically drunk and many diabetics have died because people in the street think they're drunk and don't bother to try and help them. I had diabetes when I was 14, when my mother died. Perhaps it was the shock of her death or maybe it was because of all the sugary drinks she had bribed me with to dance with her to try to win my father back. No-one really knows what causes diabetes.

When I came round, a Chinese nurse was standing over me, fiddling with a glucose drip which fed a needle in the back of my hand. It hurt. A badge clipped to her breast read "May Ling, Diabetic Ward, Charing Cross Hospital." So there it was. I had lost another skirmish in the battle to ignore my condition.

"Welcome back, Mr. Barty."

"What happened to me?" I had been in hospital before of course and I knew that, if beds were available, they would want to keep me in there for a few days. I wanted to convince her that I was completely recovered and ready to leave.

"An ambulance brought you in." She took out a blood glucose monitor and took one of my fingers and pricked it, placing the bead of blood on the test-strip. "It's still low. We may want to keep you in here for a few days."

"But..."

"We'll see what the doctor says. You've been a silly boy," She frowned. "Our resources are over-stretched here, so she may let you go." She giggled. "Maybe you can charm her."

She stood up. "There's a relative of yours outside. Your uncle."

Uncle Audley's protruding stomach appeared at the doorway under his usual loudly flamboyant waistcoat, his white hair dishevelled and his pink face grim.

"Dear Boy. I'm not pleased. I've decided to discontinue those courses. Health and Safety…"

"Yes, I'm fine thanks. How are you Uncle?"

He drew a chair towards the bed and sat his loud bulk down. "I spoke to Anna Bullock. She has never seen anything like that before. I've asked her for a full report."

"What happened? I mean apart from my hypoglycaemia?" My head felt like an egg in a frying pan, hard outside and all hot and runny inside.

"Well, it wasn't what any of us expected, that's for sure." Uncle Audley smirked, "I didn't realise that you were a religious sort, spouting it at the top of your voice like that. If you want, you could become a full-time member of the Institute." The smirk went. "We have a very good library, you know, now that you have got nothing better to do."

It was his polite way of saying he was disappointed. He was always, and always had been, scrupulously polite. His reminder made me recoil. But he was right of course. I had reached rock bottom. Broke, divorced, ill, hospitalised, alone. I had failed all his expectations and had spat his generosity and help back in his face. The generosity and support he had given me all his life.

"I'm sorry, Uncle."

"Well, something good came out of it. That girl. Zana Sokoli. I've asked her to do some work for the Institute. She wants to speak to you."

"What about? What did you say?"

"I gave her the key to your barge and she's gone over."

"What did you do that for?" Panic. Visions of old washing, old dishes, beer cans, half-empty and half-full bottles of gin, whisky and filthy chaos, all contained in a nine-foot wide, sixty-foot long rusting steel box floating above the Thames mud. I recalled the elegant dress and her straight back. Her beauty, if I was honest. She would be long gone when I got back. Christ, it was all there, Lionel Barty on a plate, all laid out like an dead insect pinned out and ready for dissection. And then there was Dek and his girls in the boat next door. Shit.

"Time to clean up before it's too late, my boy." Uncle Audley reached into the side-cupboard and took out a hospital Bible with a lime-green sick-proof plastic cover. "You could start with this little book. It's still quite a good read in parts, you know. You obviously know some of it by heart."

"Never read it." I was still thinking about Zana.

My uncle's expression changed. An idea which he didn't want me to see and he tried to hide, "Are you sure of that?"

"Yes – never read it."

"Strange," He said.

"Why?"

"Because when you were at Anna Bullock's session, you know, channelling that girl Zana's father, you quoted from it at the top of your voice before you collapsed."

"Which bit?"

"You yelled out it out, word for word......Some of it in English, some in Albanian," He looked at me slowly, still trying to decide if I was lying or not. "Yes. That girl Zana said she recognised the words you spoke in Albanian."

"I have never heard any Albanian, apart from a few words which Dek says occasionally. I couldn't have done that. It's impossible. What was it I said?"

Audley shrugged and looked out of the window at the Hammersmith skyline. He was pretending to be unconcerned, I could see. He was thinking. Then he decided to give it to me straight.

"My boy. What you blurted out was a passage from *The Book of Revelations*."

11

Tirana

As night fell the air became cooler, but the pavements of Vaso Pasha Street were still hot to the soles of his shoes as Sokoli walked into the Block district. It was the hour of the *Xhiro*, the Albanian's evening promenade that began in twilight and continued well into the night. He felt an acute estrangement from the place and the people, as if it were a foreign country where he didn't speak the language. The place was full of bars, cafés, karaoke joints and noise and lights. Groups of newly-rich city kids spilled out of bars, dressed in the latest, many with silly American-style baseball caps, double parking their expensive cars along the street. Less fortunate groups of teenagers strolled arm-in-arm, round and round in an endless promenade, the girls wearing trousers and skirts well below their hip-bones. The Block area, formerly exclusive to the Dictator and the politburo, had been completely overtaken by showy development. Cigarette-sellers parked their wheeled metal cabinets on every corner, dogs and illicit euro-sellers lounged in the shadows and the deep bass thud of amplifiers came from the inside of every building, clashing or chiming in with the petrol-generators. Down precipitous steps, basement shops sold clothes, rows of CDs, mobile telephones and second-hand paperback books. Families sat in amongst giggling and shrieking students and dark rugged men in sinister leather coats. Oblivious to the chaos, two bald and bearded old men were sitting on folding stools at the edge of the pavement, quietly absorbed in a game of chess on an upturned cardboard box. Above, tall office buildings housed agencies, lawyers, accountants, tax and investment advisers and estate agents, all no doubt now on the lower levels having their first pre-dinner drinks after a profitable day in the office.

Sokoli nearly lost his way as he tried to recognise the old landmarks. The Dictator's house he recognised, set back from the road. The high walls were still there, but it had become a language school and a smart restaurant and club, one which Sokol could not possibly afford to eat in, even if they had let him in. Maybe when he had finished this, he too would have a new life and forget the past altogether. Maybe he would meet someone, a nice Muslim lady, someone kind and a good cook, and they would be able to stroll the streets in the evening and enjoy themselves. He would change into somebody else.

He could recognise his bearings now. He turned left and then along the street a bit, then right into a quiet unlit street away from the noise. Halfway down there was a broad steel gate and outside were two men waiting in the dark mauve shadows of an overhanging eucalyptus tree. Neither of them spoke as Sokoli drew out the precious bunch of keys from his pocket and turned the largest of them in the lock. They silently nodded as he went in and drew the gate shut behind him.

Nothing had changed apart from the overgrowth. The dark garden was now completely overgrown, but he remembered the way well. A two-foot steel door at the back lead down to three sets of deep basements. It opened easily as he unlocked it and crept down the steel stairs towards the Quiet Room. Another steel door opened with a rush of fetid air and he went inside.

He stopped and looked in. Everything was the same, abandoned in 1985 when the Dictator had breathed his last paranoid breath and after the project had been forgotten ten years earlier. Wooden shelves from wall to ceiling were stacked with carefully labelled slim cardboard sleeves containing aluminium discs. To Sokoli they were shelves full of the voices of corpses. How many people had suffered in here, gone deaf or mad and then been thrown out into the camps and the work gangs? With a dreadful irony, he remembered that most were sent off under guard to Mount Daijti, up in the Northern Albanian Alps, to mine bauxite and create more aluminium, a lot of which had been used for the project. Starved and freezing, completely disposable, they were forced without any special clothing apart from the rags they wore to mine, sort and then heat bauxite in a pressure vessel along with sodium hydroxide at a temperature of double boiling point. At these temperatures, the bauxite dissolved as an aluminate and then, after separation and discarding of the red mud, seeded with aluminium hydroxide. The mineral had then been dissolved at a temperature of about 960 °C in molten cryolite and electrolysed. Hardly any men or women had survived. He had been one of the very few. The lives and resources used to create this venture had been squandered on the whim of a madman. The project had not worked. The equipment was not good enough. The theory had failed. All that remained were the rows and rows of recordings on out-of-date and rudimentary aluminium discs. At the time, because of the cost of the process, these discs had been more expensive than gold.

He gazed up at the rows of shelves. He thanked Allah that he had had the strength and will to survive the mines himself so he still had time to try and get back the one person he wanted. Needed.

Sokoli stole forward between the archives to a cupboard in the corner. It had two locks and he used his remaining two keys to open it. At the back, hidden, was another steel door with a German combination lock. Sokoli turned the lock-wheel back and forth and he was relieved to know it had not jammed. He spun it in the set sequence that he remembered from so long ago. Inside, he found the expected thick brown plastic case. In fading ink, it was marked "Dora Zygari. 1976". In it was a thin cardboard dossier, a wide spool of magnetic recording tape, just one aluminium disc and two twelve-inch shellac discs. And a photograph.

The photograph was grainy monochrome and showed a pretty dark-haired woman in a yard with stone walls which were scarred by bullet-holes. She wore what looked like gypsy dress with a polka-dot scarf wrapped tightly round her head. She looked straight at the camera with an expression which he could not look at for long without turning away. A Sigurimi police officer stood slightly behind her holding a rifle to her head. He was smiling and his finger was on the trigger.

Sokoli gathered up the dossier, the spool and the two discs and the photograph, put them back carefully in the plastic case and turned back. He paused outside the locked door to the Quiet Room, more in quiet remembrance than anything else. He didn't want to go in, even if he had had the key he wouldn't have wanted to enter. This was the room which had been designed so that it was completely silent, so that any sound made was completely pure and ear-drums could be manipulated or burst, the aural nerves to the brain played with and monitored at leisure.

He locked all the doors and left, the way he had come in, across the overgrown garden. He nodded to the two men outside, locked the gate and made his way across the Block to the lawyer's house to deliver the goods.

12

London

After Uncle Audley left, I discharged myself from Charing Cross. There was some disapproval, but the doctor didn't argue too much. Of course, I realised, they needed the bed for another patient.

It was good to get out in the air after the hospital. I needed some time to think, but I also needed a change of clothes, so I had to go back to the barge. I took the slow river route along the walkway by the Thames toward Hammersmith Bridge, the tide on the ebb. I strolled by the River Café and looked inside at the wealthy, eating lunch, just as I had done with my record company clients in a time which I could now only dimly remember – egocentric musicians, jealously comparing royalty rates, advertising budgets and press, unscrupulous executives, contracts endlessly renegotiated, reneged upon and re-drafted and the late nights and the talk and the alcohol. I felt happier now. Broke, yes, but happier.

I had to get my act together. A common expression, but it has a different significance when you have Asperger's syndrome. Because we with it have our brains wired differently from normal – that's the theory anyway. I had never been able to relax in people's company and had always felt better alone. Other people drained me. After two hours in any gathering – a social event, business meeting or whatever – my concentration would evaporate and my mind would curl up in its safe shell and drift away, like a snail floating along in a gentle sun-dappled stream. After two hours I just had to escape from whoever it was I was with. If that was impossible, any time after that was exhausting because I couldn't keep up the concentration. We with the condition therefore are noted for not making eye-contact and not being socially aware. We live in our closed minds, letting in only what is proven, interesting and fascinating. Well there isn't usually very much that is interesting or fascinating in everyday life with normal people. My poor wife had tried her best, bless her, but then it all got too much for her. I didn't blame her for it and still loved her, really, underneath it all. She was normal. I wasn't. Simple as that.

So, because of all these difficulties, I had developed a system of acting a rôle. I would look carefully at any forthcoming meeting, who would be there and so on, what I wanted from it and them, and adopt a ready-prepared persona to fit it. Like a detective policeman must do in preparing for an interview with a witness or a suspect. I believe I am good at this. Sometimes there are surprises, but I usually meet them with a good dose of unrehearsed charm – something I had seen in normal people and copied. A reliable technique for this was to get people to talk about themselves (usually very easy) and punctuate their replies with short expressions of interest, encouragement or sympathy. This was relaxing, because you could do it when only half out of your shell and took no real effort.

But there was no rôle prepared for me now. I naturally hoped that the girl Zana was *not* at the barge, but if she was going to be there she would probably be morose after the session and would want to talk about her problems, worse her feelings, over endless cups of tea without a proper drink in sight. I sat down on a bench on the high concrete Thames embankment, watched the river and the passers-by with their dogs and tried to anticipate as best I could. I stretched my legs out and rested my head on the back of the bench and looked up into the big fat cumulus clouds above the river. At times like these this was helpful, as I could see a thousand stories and characters up there, ever changing as the early-afternoon sun stretched across the white vapour, creating ever changing highlights, depths and shadows. I could see Valkyrie horsemen, bearded heroes, goblins with expressions of love, delighted laughter, doubt, worry, remorse and hate. I could see lost souls from Hogarth etchings of gin alley, gremlins, demons, sprites and gnomes, some in convoluted groups of huddled and urgent discussion, some in lonely contemplation. Soft maidens, their white loins spread out in ecstatic and tender masturbation of their deeply shadowed pubis, faces thrown back and raised to the sun, were tended by a gloating deep-eyed homunculi whose expression altered in the light from tender concern to laughter in an unfolding tableau of lust. It was an endless, ever-changing story, a cartoon drawn by a master of light and shade. Then, two dogs started a fight on the tow-path and the sun went in and it was all gone.

I brought my mind back from the vanished stories to my problem. I could see there would be an awkward introduction, a first cup of tea, a lot of silence and a great deal of useless and inconclusive whining about a terrible disaster which nobody could do anything about. No doubt, Zana was suffering. But I couldn't see the point – why had she asked to come over? I decided I would listen for a bit, ask her about herself, try and show some sympathy and roll it along until the two-hour limit was up and then get rid of her, have a large whisky and go to sleep. I could eat later. I had some burgers and a few potatoes left.

My barge was moored just under The Blue Anchor by Hammersmith Bridge, the third boat out from the bank. I had been very lucky to rent it cheap. It needed a lot of maintenance which I could not afford and I had heard that one of the steel hull plates below the water needed replacing. But it was home, at least for the moment. To reach it, I had to cross over two other barges, the closest one owned by someone I had never seen and the middle one occupied by Dek. Dek had moved into his boat just after me but his was much more expensive. The river tide here was still just after turning on the ebb and the water was still deep. The gangway could be treacherous, so I crept across gingerly. My hand on the rail was still hurting from the glucose drip in the hospital.

Dek and three of his girls were standing at the stern of his barge looking down into the engine well. Dek saw me and waved, "Asparagus!" For some reason, he could never remember the word "Aspergers", a syndrome I had confessed I might have one late night in the Nook of The Blue Anchor. "How are you? I hear you been into the hospital?"

Dek had no notion that I might want my condition kept secret. This was a symptom of his own frankness. He was about forty years of age, dark-hair curly, short and well-built with a muscular frame. To see his brown eyes you had to look under the ledge above them, the jut of his frontal cranium, where they were deeply recessed, deeply set. If one didn't know him, he would look foreign and frightening. When you got to know him, though, you would get to know a kind man, an accomplished musician. He was also a sado-masochistic night club owner. By this, I mean an owner of a sado-masochistic night-club, not a sado-masochistic owner of a night-club. It wasn't in Soho, as you might expect. It was near Parliament Square and catered mostly for politicians and civil servants. The club was doing well. It was close enough to Westminster for the Division Bell. He was looking to expand. He was thinking of setting up another one and had plans for going into the manufacture of sex toys. But he knew nothing at all about diesel engines.

The three girls looked up from the engine well as I stepped onto the very wide side-deck of Dek's boat. I was so used to his girls, I didn't even notice their dress, but it would, I suppose, have looked strange to the uninitiated lunchtime drinkers on the terrace of The Blue Anchor. But, hey, this was London. One, Maureen, blonde with gray eyes, who had a strong Welsh lilt, wore a creamy see-through dress so tight and short it barely hid anything. Maisie, brunette crop with a fringe from Dorset, wore a red latex jump-suit which must have been very hot and, I couldn't help thinking, not a little unhygienic. Then Sally (Glasgow, Scotland) was a red-head and skimpily dressed as a private school-girl, complete with panties, stockings and suspenders which she made sure everyone could see. They all wore spiked dog-collars round their necks. Dek had a cunning radio transmitter attached by a silver chain to his black pirate leather shorts, by which means he could send a small electric shock to a receiver built into the dog-collars, when he felt a non-verbal admonishment was needed. The girls loved each other and adored Dek. Dek's boat was about twice the size of mine and the girls slept together in a metal cage below-decks in the prow. Dek had occasionally offered his girls to me, as a gesture of neighbourly friendship, as you might offer to lend your lawnmower, but I couldn't see myself carrying it through, so to speak. They all had hearts of gold and the girls were really very kind and I actually felt a little bit sorry for them all and their dependency. I really didn't feel like the offered blow-job. I would have been embarrassed. When you got Dek onto the subject of sex (which was fairly easy at any time) he would go on and on and on about it, obsessed, relentless, not realising how tedious it became to the listener – at least after the first half-hour. It was all so *biologically mechanical*, the way he told it. But then, I had Asperger's and I had also been married. So romantic illusion wasn't really an arrow in my quiver. I put it down to a lack of hormonal equilibrium – theirs, not mine.

You see, I have a confession which may or may not interest you, but I'll explain it anyway. I find that the manipulation of women is far more interesting than the women themselves. Take, for example, Dek's girls. Sure, there must be reasons for their odd inclinations, but any investigation of that would be straightforward, pretty much cause and effect. There was no mystery, they held no devils, no enigma, no riddle.

What was really alluring was the pretty young woman who had devils in her, who could therefore be slowly teased out to tell her story and in the process of confession, her trust gained over time, manipulated and seduced. This was the great game. It was a little bit like cloud-watching. Yes, you may say, that's cruel, he's all head and no heart. But the heart could follow, eventually, I always hoped. It had nearly happened with my wife, nearly. But she had rumbled me and once that happened I lost interest, she felt it and we began to coexist. Then she lost interest and the rest you know.

Dek was conscious of his duty of confidentiality to his clients, but without naming names would tell me the most extraordinary stories. He had a cosy relationship with MI6 who could get hold of him at any time in cases of emergency. My favourite was the story of a junior minister who had been summoned to Heathrow from the club at short notice. He had, in his rush, forgotten the thin chain locked to his ankle by which he had been secured to a naked whip-holding barmaid who had lost the key in all the excitement. Dek had been 'phoned in the middle of the night from MI6 in Vauxhall and had had to go to Heathrow airport with the key to unlock the minister from the barmaid before his flight.

People paid a lot of money to be able to spend their time carrying out their secret fantasies in a safe environment. Dek's attitude was safely avuncular and he had, as a result of his club activities, seen virtually every form of kinkiness which existed and was a pretty good psychologist and a very good judge of human nature.

"I still think it's the alternator," Maisie put her hands on her plump latex hips and said in a Dorset burr which always made me think of *Cider With Rosie*, "It was always the alternator with my uncle's tractor. The hours I spent bending over fiddling with it." She gave me a long look.

A feminine voice came from deep down in the engine well. Calm, thoughtful. A voice I knew very clearly. "No, I am certain it's the solenoid." A head appeared, covered in a red polka dot scarf tightly wrapped, the ends sticking out, oil streaks either side of her nose. It was Zana. "Dek, have you got a socket spanner?"

13

Zana had borrowed my old blue canvas overalls, pinned the straps up and had rolled up the legs to fit. Her hair was poking out from under the scarf in rich dark tufts. Her eyes still looked as if she was thinking about the engine and the solenoid as she caught sight of me and, surprised, tried to adjust her expression. She hoisted herself out of the well with an easy movement and looked at me, her voice a little clipped and wary. "How are you feeling?"

"Fine, thanks." My reply was a bit lame, but nothing else came to mind. Without my preparations, I was forced to ad lib.

"I need to speak to you, Lionel. Could you wait while I just finish this?"

Dek handed Zana a spanner and she dropped back down into the hatch. He looked at me a little longer than he usually did. "Isn't she the most beautiful mechanic in the…." He searched for an appropriate word, "vicinity?" I knew what he was really thinking. I was thinking it too.

I went across the last duck-board to my boat. The stern doors were wide open and I went down the steep wooden steps, filled a kettle with water and put it on the gas hob. Outside, I heard Dek's engine start with a few coughs and a rumble and then heard a cheer from his girls.

I peeked into the shower-room. As you would expect, I hadn't cleaned it for months. I stood there and pondered my reflection in the half-light. Corn-coloured hair still curly, good and strong, good chin, green eyes a bit closed in and sad. Altogether, not bad, considering. Shave needed.

I heard feet jumping down the steps. The kettle started its breathy whistle on the hob.

Zana poked her head round the door and looked at me. "I think I need something stronger than tea."

I offered to take her to The Blue Anchor, but she declined and said she wanted to be alone with me.

"Lionel, would you mind if we clear a space?"

I nodded at the reproach. She had seen the way I lived. I duly cleared the old bottles and discarded clothing and made a space by the wood-burner. She went, rather gingerly I thought, into the shower-room and changed out of my overalls and her head-scarf and came back wearing a white t-shirt and black trousers, black plimsolls, a light-green cardigan over her shoulders. She had brushed her hair. She didn't seem to be wearing make-up. From her big saddle-brown leather handbag she brought out a bottle of riaki, poured two glasses and handed one to me. She went back down the cabin, shut the cabin door and came back and sat down by the wood-burner. I sat on the other chair.

"After what happened at the Institute, I came here to tell you a story. I'll be as clear as I can and it may sometimes sound like fantasy," She looked up, "But please bear with me. I think you may be able to help me." She took a sip of the riaki.

That voice of hers. I could listen to her recite a gas bill reminder or one of my dwindling bank statements and not care about anything. I settled back in my chair, sipped the riaki and felt its warm glow. Zana was certainly very beautiful. That sounds trite and I'll rephrase. She had a quality of rich depth, her voice moving warm and fluid like the faint movement on the surface of a mill pond, a ruffled cadence made charming by her hesitancy. This was promising, auspicious. If it wasn't, I wouldn't have to engage with her and I was pretty sure it wouldn't take more than two hours. But it sounded full of promise. I composed my features into my warm face, replete with empathy and understanding, and waited for her to begin, trying to keep my eyes on hers and not to look at her legs. But when she spoke, I felt drawn in again, irresistibly, her deep tonal inflection drew me into her story like a wasp to an open jar of honey, or, I imagined, as a pollen-bee to the nectar-hard stamen in the cleft of an open flower. But I digress.

14

"I was born in Albania at the time of the communist dictatorship there. It had lasted for 40 years since the Second World War. The dictator had closed the country and nobody could enter or leave without official permission."

"After the communism began, Albania was declared an atheist country - all religions were banned and were declared illegal. People who were known or seen to be religious were killed. Even up there in the mountains, families who had lived together for decades began to suspect each other and old friends would betray each other. There was a reward for informers, a small one but significant to the desperately poor villagers."

"The village was high up in the Albanian mountains close to the border with Yugoslavia. A rudimentary village of stone buildings which had been there for centuries and which had a nunnery."

"My mother was a religious woman who had worked as a cook at the nunnery. She believed in ghost stories which had been told but never written down and could sing the ancient songs which she had learnt from her own mother and her aunt who had been famous singers and who had been discovered in the days of King Zog before the war and had been fêted in Tirana as the true voice of the spirit of Albania, of the ancient Illyrians, expert in the old songs which had been learnt and re-learnt way back through the generations. Zog was unpopular and had suffered more than fifty assassination attempts. He got his staff to promote my mother's aunt as a Nationalist symbol. She became fashionable, moved to Tirana. She went to Vienna with King Zog's sisters and was becoming quite an international star to the cognoscenti. But when the Italians took over and King Zog was deposed and went into exile in 1939 the two sisters – my grandmother and her sister Dora - went with him and Queen Geraldine to England where they stayed on his money at the Ritz in London. Zog had raided the National Banks before his departure, so could well afford it."

Zana slowly took another, larger, sip of riaki. "Still with me?"

I nodded. Was she making it up? It sounded like something out of *The Prisoner of Zenda*. She was an interesting mix. Sometimes I saw the vulnerability of a young girl, but then the confidence of the practical young woman would clamp down and squash the fragility and the girl would disappear. Only rarely did the two coexist in her expression.

"My father, a village boy who had joined the partisans in the war, came back to the village as a minor official of the communist secret police, called the Sigurimi. They took over the nunnery and after a while, with little else to think about apart from the Manifesto, spying on the villagers and worrying about an invasion from Yugoslavia, he asked her father for my mother's hand. He sent his own mother to the father with the usual gift, which was accepted. A matchmaker was found. Their families agreed. They married. At first it was all good, they had money, were far away from the dreadful and vicious turmoil in the cities on the plains below."

I adopted a suitable expression of concern. Zana looked at me with a touch of frustration. Then she slowed down, speaking to me with the tone of a patient professor giving a tedious explanation to a rather thick student.

"Back then, in the mountains, a woman was bought. All that Albanian men expected of their women was that they fetched wood, cooked all of the meals, baked bread and made clothes. They used the women to carry goods when their mules were ill. Get the idea? Women did all the hard work. As well as bearing and caring for the children, of course."

"Anyway, I was born, a difficult birth. Then my father found out about my mother's Aunt and started to take an interest in the local songs and legends. A curious thing happened. He became obsessed. He went to Tirana and told the Chief of the Sigurimi that he had discovered some secret songs that could be adapted for use in communist propaganda. Hearts and Minds stuff. He was promoted and it went to his head. My mother sang for him. She believed in his work. She was his wife and so she obeyed him totally as is the way up there. He even bribed the villagers into trucks and took them to Tirana to record them singing."

"He was promoted. The Dictator himself took an interest in his work. Then, full of himself, one cold night he came back to the village unexpected and found my mother reading to me in bed. In one flat minute he realised that his whole career, even his life, was in danger. She was reading from the Bible. As a Sigurimi officer he wouldn't have survived for a moment if anyone had found out."

"But Zana. That's what I saw. Isn't that what I saw at the Institute?"

"Yes. I think it must have been. But what you said must be wrong." She shook her head, "You have got to be wrong."

"How? Why?" My little plan for a long-drawn out seduction was fading fast.

"Because my grandmother would *never* have killed her daughter. It was impossible. She wasn't there and she never got over her guilt at leaving her behind in Albania. What you said in that session can't be true…Why did you…what made you say what you did?"

"I dunno." I thought back. "All I can say is that my feelings and my words came from somewhere outside of me. Maybe the whole thing's a fake." I wanted to help her, but I couldn't see how. "I don't see how I can help."

She drank, looked into her glass, shrugged, "I have nobody else to help me. I need to understand what happened."

I took another sip and used the moment to glance down at my wristwatch. She had been here more than two hours and I hadn't even noticed. The snail had been drawn out of its shell. The riaki was very strong and I was feeling it. "What happened to your mother?"

"I am not really certain what happened after that. I was only 8 years old. Some men came and I was smuggled across the border. They were British. They took me to Vienna by train where my grandmother Zana was waiting for me."

"Where is she now, your Grandmother?

"The Isle of Wight. A home in a place on the south coast called Ventnor." Zana shrugged, "She has had dementia for several years."

Christ! Why couldn't everything go to plan? The coincidence was far too strong to be one. The riaki heat left me and I felt cold. "My father lives in Ventnor," I blurted.

The snail was retreating into its shell, for its own protection. The dappled stream had become a river, swelled to a flood and the waters were choppy under the chill of an eastern wind.

I needed something to eat.

I am quite a resourceful cook, I think. I had some burgers which were still good and the potatoes only had tiny green buds growing out of them. I boiled, then fried, the chopped potatoes in sunflower oil and added some tomatoes and garlic to the burgers as they fried in butter and olive oil. I added soya sauce to a tin of baked beans and added some parsley which wasn't too old to eat. I found a 1998 bottle of French merlot from a good grower which had been a gift from a grateful client.

I found some clean plates and cutlery. Zana didn't complain about the food. We talked for a long time. I felt myself opening up. I was completely honest with her about myself. Against her story, my problems shrank into insignificance. I was no longer entirely the centre of my own attention.

She had lived in England under the protection of her grandmother since she was little. Her grandmother had been a very strong woman, but she suffered. She had harboured a bitterness. Her sister, Dora, was the more beautiful and had a much better singing voice. Grandmother Zana had been more plain, more work-a-day. Before Zog abdicated, she had given birth to Zana's mother. She had told Zana that Zog was the father and that she was therefore a princess. She had never spoken the word *illegitimate*. Zana's mother was, as a child, left in the village under the care of the nuns. When the two sisters left the country with Zog and his small retinue, they thought it was for a few weeks and Grandmother Zana meant to return. In fact, Zog had never returned and after the War the communists had taken over and their steel grip on the country would last for another 40 years. Many years later, my Zana was born with a Sigurimi officer as a father and the rest you know. I am only saying "my Zana" to differentiate the two, I hope you understand.

Finding that the British after the end of the war considered him to be an irrelevant anachronism in the new world order, Zog left England. He tried to leave for America, but settled for Egypt. But he had made provision for the two sisters. They lived together for a long time, but then Dora was invited back to Albania by the Communists and, to her sister's consternation, she accepted. Although Zog had tried to help her in England to forge a career, it had come to nothing. Disappointed, she was easily enticed back to Albania by promises of becoming a national emblem of the new State, of records, fame and money and the proximity of Italy across the Strait of Otranto. The two sisters never spoke again.

Dora Zygari then disappeared, like many people in Albania at the time.

Having then lost her entire family, Zana's grandmother had asked the British government to help and they had agreed and had got young Zana out via Yugoslavia to Vienna, where grandma Zana had met her and taken her back to England. Why the British government had helped, Zana didn't know and it had remained one of her Grandmother's secrets. Secrets which were now probably lost forever. Ironically, of course, if they had waited a few more years, the regime would have collapsed and the Albanian borders opened to everyone.

"Did she make a will?"

"Yes, definitely, she told me. But I am not to see it until she dies. Even now I am not one of her attorneys because of the dementia. There are trustees of the estate."

"Who?"

"I won't know that either, until she dies. Or…when my 30th birthday comes."

"Who runs her interests now?"

"The trustees."

I realised that I knew nothing about her at all. "What do you actually do, Zana? What's your full name? Where do you live?"

She sort of grinned. But her attempt at grinning was odd, as if her grinning muscles were unused and slack. It was the first time I had seen Zana try to look remotely happy. "That took you a long time." She considered her answer, "I work in advertising, I'm a planner. Freelance. I live in Haverstock Hill in a beautiful flat owned by the trustees. Unfortunately, I share it with someone I detest, she's called Joanna, whom I am trying my best to get rid of. She was let in by the managing agent with the consent of the trustees but without consulting me. She's horrible. The type who will help herself to your food, complain about the state of the kitchen, cook your food without offering you any of it and then leave dirty pots and plates all over the kitchen for you to clear up before the next time she deigns to eat your food." Zana paused and sighed, "And then she'll watch a TV show which I don't like and munch her way through until it's over. But getting through to the trustees is difficult and they will only communicate through a dragon of personal assistant for whom I only have an email address. To tell you the truth, I don't spend much time in the flat. Joanna is a little intrusive, she would have made a good parking attendant or a policewoman. Very silly and very annoying. If my grandmother knew what was going on she would give them all hell" She recovered herself, "But then I suppose if she knew what was going on, they wouldn't be there. Anyway, my full name is Zana Maria Sokoli. I'm 29." She looked up and sensed my question, "And, no, I'm not married and I don't have a boyfriend."

"What does a planner do?"

Zana looked a little bit miffed at my question. She breathed in and said rather curtly, "A planner plans, sees ahead, investigates and plans things so that all the others, the copywriters, art department, creatives and so on, can do a good job. So the objective can be achieved."

I hailed a taxi for her on the bridge. We exchanged numbers. I said I would call her if I could explain anything more about what I had seen. She said she would call me. As the taxi pulled away, her expression looked a little bit doubtful when she waved back at me.

I walked back down the steps from the bridge in the evening light. The Blue Anchor was filling up. I sat on a bench for a long time. I had certainly found my dream girl, I thought. She had devils, she was beautiful, she was exotic, she was capable and intelligent and she was troubled. I mentally tried out a new role, tried casting myself as the white knight. It would mean I would have to clean up, broaden my shoulders and really take an interest and give some commitment. It would take some work, but didn't look impossible. I wanted to make her smile, to make her laugh. I tried to imagine her laughing, but couldn't do it. All I could see were her sad eyes.

Further along the embankment, a cyclist mounted up and rode away down the tow-path towards Chiswick. Only after the cyclist had disappeared in the half-light, I connected two images in my mind. I was pretty sure it was the Irish woman in the motorbike jacket. But of course I could have been wrong. I was getting too bound up in the mystery of Zana and her story. We Aspergics are noted for our obsessive focus, a complete concentration on detail in a narrow chain of thought, so that we often make mistakes and miss what is blindingly obvious to a normal person with a wider view. I needed and wanted to be more normal.

16

Tirana

After Sokoli had given him the briefcase, collected his large fee in cash and gone, the lawyer sat well into the night making notes, getting his thoughts in order. This client was very important and the lawyer's own fee was huge. He had done a lot of research, so that he could report the full story from the Albanian end. Working alone, locking his papers in his private safe because nobody else must know and they must be kept secret, no electronic records, no emails, no recorded evidence, he had started from the very beginning so that he understood the complete history. He picked up the copy of the original Patent Licence from which it had all begun, which gave the detail of the invention which had carried the music of the world across the globe for eighty years on hundreds of millions of thin flat round plates pressed out from shellac – made of Indian beetles' gum mixed with alcohol and black carbon.

The two Italian brothers Ganzi had set up the business in 1926 with Italian money. Giuliano Ganzi had been the technical and business brain.

Primo Ganzi had been the musical brain. Together, they built the Ganzola record label, building the brick factory and offices in Elbasan in the middle of Albania. Giuliano dealt with all pressing and distribution, while Primo went further and further afield to find music and performing artists to record on the newly developed vacuum tube amplifiers and carbon granule microphones, sending the electrical signals to an electro-magnetic disc-cutter. Giuliano Ganzi bought more microphones, more amplifiers, more cutters, more stampers, all of increasing quality and sophistication. The accounts showed large imports of shellac from India and the purchase of many tons of carbon. The factory was extended, more buildings built, more workers hired.

Primo's artists were popular, Primo's repertoire sold well. Sales of discs on the Ganzola label were booming, markets were opening up all across Europe, things looked very good. Then, in 1937, lightning struck with a double fork which lacerated the brothers and the company. One vicious fork of lightning was Primo's decision to join the Communists. The other, softer, brighter, but no less lethal, arrived in the shapely figure of the vibrant brunette singer, Dora Zygari, and her elder sister Zana, under instructions from the King himself.

Records were made. Records were sold. Dora Zygari was invited to Milan and Rome. More records were sold. She was a star in Albania and in Italy. The factory kept churning out records of her performances and made money. A lot of it. But Primo was funding the communists, secretly under the long noses of Mussolini's Italians.

Mussolini invaded in 1939, Primo was discovered and the factory closed down.

Dora Zygari sheltered under the wing of the King. Zana Zygari disappeared into the mountains to have a child. Rumours spread that the child was of King Zog.

The lawyer turned to a print from *Wikipaedia*, giving contextual background which he knew well, but could adapt and dress up in his report as his own research. He made a mental note to give a fat donation to *Wikipaedia* as soon as his full fee was paid. It had saved him hours and hours of work and he was still stunned by the incredible amount of openly available information which it had compiled and the rigour with which it was organised. As a man who had trained under the old communist judicial system with its secrecy and corruption, he gave thanks for this blessing. He condensed it down and read it over.

After Hitler invaded Czechoslovakia without notifying Mussolini in advance, the Italian dictator decided to proceed with his own annexation of Albania and delivered to King Zog in Tirana an ultimatum on March 25, 1939, demanding that it accede to Italy's occupation of Albania. Zog refused.

While King Zog broadcast to the nation that he would resist Italian occupation, people felt that they were being abandoned by their government."

On April 7 Mussolini's troops, led by General Alfredo Guzzoni, invaded Albania, attacking all Albanian ports simultaneously. The same day King Zog, his wife, Queen Geraldine Apponyi, and their infant son Leka fled for Greece, taking with them part of the gold reserves of the Albanian Central Bank."

The lawyer looked at his watch. It was five o'clock in the morning, Tirana time. London was two hours behind. It was raining. He stood up, stretched himself and went to the toilet. Soon the Block would be opening for business and another day and night of controlled debauchery. He thought about the other report, the interview with the Rat which he had recorded in a small flat in the old town of Korcha down in the South near the Greek border, after a long and bumpy ride past Lake Ohrid and through the Morava mountains.

The Rat didn't seem to mind being called the Rat, probably because it was unanswerably the right description. His light grey working coat emphasised his thin frame and rounded stoop, he had white hair pulled back across his large pink ears and his skin had never lost the pallor of decades working over a soldering iron in a protective steel wire cage in the depths of the Electrical Block at Ganzola. The lawyer knew from the Ganzola personnel files that his name was Hermann Bahri and that he was ninety-three years old. He had worked at Ganzola all his life.

The Rat had eaten throughout the interview, suspicious, nodding, picking at his sausage with thin fingers and bad teeth. He leant over his food, his long thin head bent forward. His hands moved under the head, lifting the sausage up into his mouth. The lawyer heard his own voice on the tape machine.

"There's a question I'd like to ask you, Hermann."

The Rat had looked up.

"What can you tell me about Dora Zygari?"

The Rat had stopped eating, his teeth still embedded in the sausage. He looked as if it was poisoned. His ears moved suddenly outward as he wrenched his thin jaw free, gasping for air.

"Hermann!" The lawyer's voice was raised. A chair shot back as the Rat lurched forward, "Don't have a heart attack!"

The lawyer had leaned over and began thumping Hermann on the mound of his stoop. Hermann undid the top of his work coat and loosened his tie. He grabbed a glass and drank some beer. His hands were shaking. He had looked up as if the lawyer had accused him of a crime.

"How can you ask me that?" He rasped, "I had nothing to do with it."

His eyes had gone smaller, retracting inwards beneath his ample eye-lids, watching and waiting like an animal threatened by a predator, made vulnerable and dangerous. He felt inside his pocket and brought out a crumpled blue packet of Albanian cigarettes. He lit one, breathing in the smoke, calming himself. After a few deep lungfuls, he actually smiled, holding the cigarette up in the air. "I have been smoking these for all the time I have been at Ganzola," He said, "They only stopped putting hemp in them in 1929."

"You'll never reach 90." The lawyer heard his own bad joke on the tape.

Hermann took another pull on the cigarette, "Dora Zygari." He murmured her name with quiet reverence, then, simply, "We loved her." His pink eyes filled. "Primo loved her, we all knew that. That was the ruin."

Hermann then started speaking quietly, the years rolling away, marking out the time of his story by what he knew best. "It was the time of the RCA 44A microphone. A ribbon velocity microphone, sold by RCA in 1931. It used a small ribbon which was only two inches long and two point four millimetres wide and which moved inside a magnetic field according to the difference in sound pressure on each side of the ribbon. Bi-directional. The velocity of the moving ribbon was independent of the sound frequency, producing a high-impedance signal. It had a pickup pattern like," Hermann waved his finger in the air in a figure of eight, "A figure eight toward the front and back, eliminating unwanted noise from the sides. It was sensitive. Ideal for American crooners." He laughed and took another practised draw on his cigarette, then a swig of beer. "But it was big and heavy, only for the recording studio. And it was expensive." He looked up. "But Dora made it worth it."

On the tape there was the sound of a car outside in the narrow street, but neither had paid any attention.

"Every single Lek, every single quindarka. She was worth it." The Rat took another pull, "I remember when Primo first brought Dora to see the factory," He was looking through the walls of the kitchen into the past, "The big Lancia drew up, yes. An Astura Series 4 Pininfarina Cabriolet. Beautiful. Primo got out and held the door. I tell you, the whole factory went quiet. Dora got out. She just stood there and the whole place went quiet. The men came out of the plant and just stood there, watching her. But that was long before the regime."

Hermann stubbed his cigarette out on the floor. "Dora Zygani. She had the voice of an angel."

"What happened?" The lawyer heard his own whisper on the tape.

"She was a Sinti." He gulped some beer, "A gypsy. From the mountains in the North. She ran away with the king to the West. Then a long time after, under the communists, she came back and we did the experiments in the Quiet Room. We didn't have the equipment, though. And the experiment didn't work. But they couldn't let her talk about it, you see, to anyone. Couldn't let her leave the country."

Hermann's voice dropped two levels. He mumbled. What came out on the tape-recorder sounded like a throw-away remark.

"So they killed her."

Part Three

Discovery

17

London

"Lionel."

Dek was shaking my shoulder gently. He waited until I had opened my eyes and put a cup of tea on the ledge by my bed. The porthole showed a dark day, clouded over. I could hear the rumble of early morning traffic on the bridge and light fingers of rain on the steel roof of the barge.

"Lionel," Dek sat down on the edge of the bunk, "Your wife gives me a call. Your phone is switched off." He was looking at me uncertainly from under his bony eyebrows and took a deep breath.

I felt the throb of the riaki as I rubbed the sleep from my eyes. "Why? What does she want?" My ex-wife hadn't been in touch for at least a year. I groped for the cup and took small sips of the tea.

"Lionel. It is your Dad. I'm sorry to say your father has gone and died. Your wife. She gets a call on the land line at your, her, house from the police. They need to get contact with you. The number I have here." He handed me a piece of paper. "She said she sorry. No, she has no need to talk to you. Can I do anything for you?"

"No thanks, Dek, I'll deal with it." I sounded stronger than I felt.

"Come and have some of the breakfast if you are needing it."

After he had crept quietly up the gangway steps out into the rain, I slowly found some clean clothes and boiled an egg and made some toast and coffee. The shock and the night dehydration of the riaki made it difficult to think or move. I should have had a shower but I couldn't be bothered. Anyway, it would have taken about an hour for the calorifier to heat the water tank.

I switched on my mobile phone and rang the number. A woman's voice answered, the island accent thick with honeyed sunshine, "Shanklin police, how may I help you?"

She put me through to Inspector Brookhill. After condolences, he said that he needed to see me about a few matters which he wanted to talk to me about face to face. Could I come to the Island? We made an appointment for that afternoon. He would come over to Dad's flat in Ventnor. He gave me directions from Shanklin station, saying I could get a rail ticket from Waterloo which covered the whole journey, including the ferry from Portsmouth to Ryde Pier and then the train from Ryde Pier to Shanklin. He suggested I buy a monthly return ticket, as I may have to stay on the Island for a while.

I rang Audley. Twilda Tonlinson answered and told me he was abroad on business. I left a message. It was a short message. Dad had died and I would need a small loan to cover my trip. Twilda was silent for a bit. "My Dear, I'm so sorry, but remember the mustard seeds." Twilda's voice was unusually gentle. After a moment I recognised what she was talking about, one of Audley's Buddhist stories about a woman whose only child had died and became so desperate with sorrow she had already nearly lost her mind. The Buddha gave her a brass bowl and told her that before he could agree to bring the child back to life, she must take the bowl from house to house and fill the bowl with mustard seeds, one from each family where no one had died. She went from house to house, but returned with an empty bowl. She could not find a house which had not suffered the death of a family member. She understood that there is no house free from death.

I thanked Twilda, of course. I tried to feel some emotion but all I could manage was solemn resignation, if I'm honest. There was no guilt, remorse, grief or sadness, the things I had heard that normal people feel when one of their parents dies. I busied about and packed a few things. A suit and a nearly clean shirt. I went into the shower-room to get my toothbrush and razor. On the stool were my old blue canvas overalls, stained with oil. My phone went off with an unwelcome shrillness. It was Zana's number. I told her my news.

"You must be feeling rotten. Can I do anything?" Her cut-glass accent held a warmth I hadn't heard before – she sounded genuinely concerned. I tried to think of something she could do, something I could ask which would keep us in contact. Then she volunteered the answer that I couldn't have asked her for.

"I would like to come with you," She said, "I could visit my grandmother as well. Would you mind that?"

18

I wrapped my scarf tighter around my neck, my cocoon of emptiness. The train, partly cleaned by the half-hearted efforts of the cleaners, was nearly empty as it crept out from the shadows of the massive London Waterloo station. The morning sun broke through. Zana came over and sat next to me, facing the engine. We trundled through South West London, stopping at one inner city station after another, then out into the Surrey suburbs towards the coast.

"I love trains." Zana said, in good heart. It was nice to see her in a good mood, "I feel, sort of, out of time. You have a future on a train, going somewhere new, as if anything could happen to you." She looked at me, suddenly leant over and kissed me. "What did he do, what did your father do, Lionel?"

I was shocked by the kiss. I suppose it was sympathy, that Zana expected me to feel things that I wasn't feeling. But it was a relief to talk about my father. Maybe by talking about him to her, I would start to feel normal feelings about him. "He was a PRS man."

"What's that? The PRS?"

I took refuge in a long-winded explanation. "The PRS is the Performing Right Society. It will collect all your music public performance royalties for any radio, TV, internet or live playings. Worldwide. It's what musicians call "publishing" and it's automatic. All you have to do is register the songs and the splits and sit back and wait for the money to roll in."

"Splits? What are splits?"

"The share of the song you get if the song is co-written by you with others. It's calculated in twelfths." I shrugged, "Don't ask me why."

"PRS man." Zana looked out the window at the backs of the houses slipping by as we headed South. "Sounds like a secret policeman, or an agent."

"He was, kind of, in a very small way."

When my father had spoken at all, he told me that his job was ridiculous, but that he ate and drank well. For a pittance plus expenses, passing as one of the crowd in a permanently tarnished old mac, he sat in cafés, restaurants and bars waiting for the jukebox, the radio or a CD to play for the customers. He would then ask for the manager and ask politely if the proprietor had a music licence. Sometimes, unbelievably, they had a licence and he would thank them and be on his way. But usually they had no music licence and Dad would have to break through the laughter or hostility and patiently explain that, under the Copyright Act, it was illegal to play copyright music in public without a licence from the PRS. He would show his card and deal with the disbelief, resentment or anger, make a report and collect the licence fee. Sometimes they would throw him out, with the added complication of a grazed arm, a call for the police and yet more paperwork.

Dad had survived the war by being in the Royal Observer Corps and, as far as I could remember, had been depressed ever since. My mother had rarely talked to me about my father. Much younger than him, she had met him in a café in Cowes where she worked as a waitress. The marriage had been a mistake. Mum had been a pretty but frail girl, a German war refugee brought up in a Barnardo's home, keeping up a brave and smiling face in post-war Britain against the suspicion and prejudice caused by her accent. She was willing to throw in her lot with an older man and I assumed as I looked back that she had been fired by a desperation for security. But she had been drowned by his silence. I had been spawned in her desperation, a last gasp. My mother had decided that if they had a child, things would get better. Things didn't.

"Mum died when I was fourteen. The PRS finally retired Dad early on a tiny pension. He moved from one seedy flat to another until he finally could go no further. To where we're headed."

"I know where we're going, Lionel." Zana reached over and held my hand. I felt incredibly discomfited by this and didn't know how to act. I liked her a lot, but I didn't like *it*. Not yet, anyway. I didn't want to offend her, but my natural reaction was to firmly grip her hand and kiss her but I knew this was too much, too soon, so I kept my hand sort of half-limp on hers and looked out of the window, wishing she would take her hand away. She was too close and I wasn't ready. The train stopped at Woking. Everyone on the crowded platform was on their mobile telephones, either talking or plugged in, skimming the small screens with their fingers. Men, women, girls, boys, station attendants. Everyone. If I had come down from Mars, I would get the impression that here was a race locked from each other in happy isolation, each in tune with a higher being, only able to communicate through this strange medium. Odd. I'd never thought of it like that before. Somehow,

I thought they all looked like sitting ducks. As the train moved off, I took my hand away from Zana's and stood up and walked down the aisle to the toilet. I was feeling sweaty and a little bit queasy.

19

The Portsmouth ferry terminal was jam-packed, crawling with young people wearing wellington boots and carrying rucksacks and tents. It was the Isle of Wight pop festival. The queue ran all the way back to the station platform.

"My God, why do they do it?" muttered Zana as she took my hand and marched to the front of the queue. It was a very un-English thing, of course, and I was stifled by embarrassment, but no-one objected and we got on the big white catamaran without anyone complaining. Seeing her do that, the way she did it, I saw that Zana had that gift of assumed authority, an aura of precedence. I wondered how she had that, where she had got it from. On board, we went to the stern and up the stairs to the sun-deck and leant over the rail, looking down at the festival-goers filing onto the boat like refugees.

"Sheep." Zana had a funny look, her face set in contempt.

"They're only enjoying themselves, Zana."

We hardly spoke all the way on the catamaran. The sun shone and the sea breeze was fresh with the speed of the craft. I felt that symbolic sensation of escape as the Island grew near. The train met us at Ryde Pier – a 1960's London Underground train which had been poached from Northern Line duties and painted and which rattled and jerked its way down the Eastern side of the Island to Shanklin. There, the small red-brick station marked the end of the line. The sun shone strongly and the light was much cleaner than in London. An elderly Indian couple sat behind the counter of the news-stand and served coffees to the ancient hippies who sat at tables outside gossiping, smoking roll-up cigarettes, their long white hair and beards accentuating their mahogany faces. It was completely quiet save for the jingle of enamelled coloured bracelets as they raised their cups and cigarettes to their mouths and the soft banter between the hippies and a couple of taxi-drivers who waited rather aimlessly in the sunshine in the parking spaces outside the station.

"You aw-roight?" I recognised the universal Island greeting, "Turned out fine again, as they say in Arabia!" The taxi-driver was looking at Zana with barely-disguised awe, hoping we would hire him. With equally barely-disguised pride, I shook my head at the taxi-driver and we went to the bus stop. The bus took us through Shanklin and south to Ventnor through the steep hills and rolling woodland and then we saw the sea.

Ventnor is a Victorian sea-side resort with little streets piled up on the side of a steep and massive hill called St. Boniface Down. Facing south, the little town gets the sun all day long and the vegetation is lush. The landlord met us at the small solicitors' office in the High Street, up from by the Esplanade. The landlord was busy. Dad had paid his rent up to the end of the month, so I could leave his things until then, otherwise he would have to chuck them out. He gave me the keys to my father's flat and left.

The solicitor looked at Zana and me, trying to work out if we were lovers. He was matter of fact. He had Dad's will and read it out quickly in the wheezy monotone of a hardened smoker, anxious to get on. "He warned me that he had never spoken to you about this, but no doubt you will have time to consider your inheritance. He has left everything to you."

Not waiting for any questions, the lawyer pressed on. "Regrettably I know no more. Now, I'll need to keep the original will for probate, but

I've made you a photocopy, Mr. Barty, your father asked that his body be cremated and I've already made the arrangements, once the Inspector has finished." the lawyer looked up, "You are the sole beneficiary, but frankly I do not expect that there will be anything remaining after my fees have been paid."

I didn't like him. "Once the Inspector has finished with what?"

"No doubt he will explain that to you when he sees you. But I believe he has asked for an autopsy."

I knew the way to the flat and automatically led Zana down Pier Street onto the street leading down to the sea. Ventnor was not as dilapidated as I remembered and it had lost the air of an out-of-date Victorian resort and I noticed that there was a lot of building going on – of smart new flats along the Esplanade. The sand looked clean and the water was blue. A fresh South-West breeze came in from the Atlantic.

The damp flat was tiny, just three small rooms above a fish and chip shop right by the sea-front wall. The inside was painted eggshell blue, the same colour as the beach huts hauled up on the shingle below. A sharp hiss of a tea urn came from the café underneath. Vinegar, cigarettes and frying batter had sent their odours upwards through the thin ceiling for decades. They reminded Zana that she was hungry. She went downstairs to the café.

I looked around the small rooms, still struggling with the revelation curtly given by the solicitor. So few things my Dad had left behind. A few clothes in a 1930s wooden veneer cupboard. A bed, bed-clothes neatly turned. A drinks cabinet. An old record turntable. A large wooden fruit crate full of black twelve-inch 78 records, each carefully wrapped in plastic. I took one of the records out of the crate and unwrapped it, slid the disc out of its paper sleeve and held it up. The twelve-inch was in perfect condition, the light shimmering out over its shiny black surface from the centre in reds and blues and violet as I turned it in my hands. I had forgotten the time just before university, just before I left, waking up in the small hours, hearing these songs from the other room as my father sat alone in the dark with a bottle, playing them over and over again.

The label was beautiful, a piece of art. Apple green, it showed a Greek nymph in gold. She wore a scarlet robe and held out an urn, dancing, as a shooting star fell in an arc above her head, her other hand clasping a partly unrolled parchment with a sign on it. The sign suggested a sort of cross, partly hidden, difficult to make out. The rest of the label was clear. *Ganzola Records. Order No. 7653. Matrix No. 2574B. "Sinti Laments" Dora Zygari* and, in the line at the circumference, *"Made in the Kingdom of Albania under licence"*.

I held the edges of the delicate black disc between my flat palms, staring at the label, turning it, watching the reds and blues and yellows of the light which seemed to pour out of the hole in the centre, as if the nymph was pouring light from the urn. Those songs. A few notes came back and I took up the tune, began to hum to myself, low, hesitantly, my voice sounding stiff and unused in my head. The songs grew and came back to me, as if heard through an overgrown wall in a forgotten garden buried in my mind. My mother's face came back. I heard her voice softly singing, saw her light cotton dress, her fair hair, felt her warmth, her smooth skin, the fragrance of her smell, the comfort of her. An ache rose in my chest and throat, a sharp pain of loss. The pain held me tight in its grip like a reproach from a trusted friend. How could I not have thought of her for so long?

Zana came back up with fried cod and chips, wrapped in newspaper, and two plastic cups of tea, dark and thick as soup. I carefully put the disc back in its sleeve and wrapper.

"Lionel, you must eat. You haven't had anything and I don't want you to collapse again." She looked really nice when she had that scolding expression.

"Zana, could you put the hot tea down and then sit down please?"

Zana put the fish and chips and tea down on the floor. She went into the small kitchen, found some forks and came out. "Is this you?" Zana stood at the kitchen door, holding up a black and white photo of me and my mother in a scuffed red leather frame, with a long gash in one side. In the photo, my mother wore an evening dress and I was squeezed into a black suit with a white shirt and a bow-tie.

"She's very pretty! And what a sweet little boy! So smart!" She teased me as she handed me the red frame.

"Mum dragged me to those dancing lessons, over and over again." I took the photo.

Zana looked up from the floor where she was now sitting cross-legged, her mouth full of cod. "Why?"

I looked at my mother's face, smiling into the camera, her fair hair tied up, an arm round my shoulder. There wasn't any sign of the anxiety which was eating her up.

"To be attractive. To offer him something to bring him back to her. She became a very good dancer, even won some prizes." I laughed. "So did I." I was still holding the disc. I thought it better to wait until I showed it to Zana. After all, it might mean nothing. No point in distracting her without a good reason. Also, I wanted some time to remember my mother as she was in the picture. I remembered her just like that, under the spinning globe in the fake evening light of some Thursday afternoon, stepping out lithe and beautiful into a well-rehearsed dance, warmed by the sunshine of an arc-light and a few carefree moments of forgetful confidence. I remembered her smile now as she held up a first prize, a gilt cup, and beckoned me over to join her in the dazzling golden light.

I had understood what was going on, but only vaguely, only at the visceral level of the early teenager. Now, looking back with some experience of life and people, I could see it clearly. I remembered that the owner of the afternoon ballroom was called Uncle Dennis who ran the Shanklin Theatre. Uncle Dennis had taken more interest in my mother's dancing and development than was appropriate. My Dad found out and, pathetically, used the only ammunition he had. He shopped Dennis's establishment to the PRS. Uncle Dennis then told my mother that my father had got up to some things during the war, including a very close relationship with a singer who had done a week at the Shanklin Theatre whilst he was in the Royal Observers, beavering away down in the basement radio control room which was linked to the huge Ventnor Radar and Radio Masts which had been built up on the top of St. Boniface Down, 800 feet above sea level. My mother lost her life-support system and the lights went out. Then the cancer had appeared and taken hold. She had died when I was fourteen and, to a large extent, I shut down too, as you know.

I ran my thumb and forefinger slowly along the gash in the red leather, back and forth, the memories flowing from the re-opened wound. Coming home one afternoon, hearing my mother shouting, I remembered the ferocity of her rage. Her shrill scorn. Something about vulgarity, her German accent heavy and guttural with emotion. She had found my father's photographs, she had said, her voice dripping with disgust. I recalled my father's mumbled voice, knowing that there was no going back.

"Why can't you forget her? You must hate us!" She had hurled the photo at his head, "It's over! Over!" The photo frame had hit the side of the enamel cooker, fallen to the floor, grazed but unbroken.

"What did you do?" Zana's voice. I hadn't realised I had been speaking.

"After Mum died, I lived with Dad until I was 18. Well, we sort of co-existed. I got a scholarship. Classics and Law. Courtesy of my Uncle." I looked up at her, a sudden clench of regret and loss squeezing the frame in my hands. "I think Dad was proud of me."

The frame came away from its backing. As I pulled at it, more photographs and a booklet slid out from the back and fell onto the floor. Zana picked them up. She stopped chewing.

"I….." She leafed through the photos, her face green under her brown skin. She choked and got to her feet, stumbled into the small bathroom.

I stood and slowly picked up the photos. Outside over the sea the clouds were full and thick, covering all but the bottom edge of a departing sun, dark and violent red, throwing out its last light beneath the raised skirts of cloud. Her rays picked out the room. Orange on egg-shell blue, my shadow against the wall.

The booklet was a printed Programme from the Shanklin Theatre from 1943, with a small tear on the cover. It was for a performance of Ivor Novello's romantic musical, *"Glamorous Night."* In a box at the foot of the Programme there was a warning in black letters:-

> **If an Air Raid Warning be received during the performance the audience will be informed. The warning will not necessarily mean that a raid will take place. Those desiring to leave the Theatre may do so, but the performance will continue.**

The show was the story of two people, a young inventor, Anthony Allen, and a glamorous operetta star, Militza Hajos, with whom he falls in love. But in fact it seemed to be a complicated story which probably could only have worked in 1935 when Novello wrote it. But then, as I read through it, it didn't seem so far-fetched, given my current circumstances. It had an uncanny resemblance to what I was going through, and to me read like a bit of a warning somehow, a premonition, as if I was an actor waiting in the wings of real life, waiting to go on stage, when the script had been changed by the unseen management and I was expected to ad lib, play life by ear. The story went like this....

Anthony Allen is disappointed with his lack of success with a new system of television (a newfangled idea, then) and, for some reason best known to himself, goes on a luxury cruise. He goes to the mythical kingdom of Krasnia, sees an operetta, *Glamorous Nights*, in which Militza Hajos, the prima-donna of the State Opera House, is singing. She is the ex-mistress of King Stefan of Krasnia.

There is an attempted assassination of Militza, prevented by Anthony, which unsurprisingly "earns him her gratitude", as it said in the Programme. By chance she joins the cruise ship on which Anthony occupies the luxury suite - which she demands. A plot is discovered to blow up the ship and kill Militza. She and Anthony escape the sinking ship. There is a "Gypsy Wedding" and a counter-plot, led by the loyal Gipsies, to restore Militza and King Stefan to public favour and defeat the revolution planned for Krasnia. Peace is achieved at the price of Militza giving up the love of Anthony and marrying Stefan; in return, the King finances Anthony's new television invention. Safely back in England, Anthony sees the first newsreel on his new television set - as the play ends he watches the Krasnian royal wedding.

It seemed a pretty harmless divertissement. I couldn't see what had upset Zana. But it was, of course, staring me in the face. She was much quicker than me. It was third down the list of characters and read:-

"Militza Hajos - an opera singer ---------Dora Zygari"

I picked up another photograph. It was a picture of my father, Jack as a young man, sitting at some sort of console in a RAF corporal's uniform writing in a ledger in the centre of a bare room surrounded by huge steel cabinets with many dials. On the back of it was pencilled "T Block". Another showed Jack standing in a room with four women in WRAF uniform, bent over desks and wearing Bakelite headphones. With him, hand on his arm, was a beautiful dark-haired woman in a long three-quarter length pleated skirt and a fur wrap who looked as if she had stepped in from a wartime cocktail party. Her full, voluptuous mouth was smiling. On the reverse of the photo, in purple-blue ink, was scribbled a note in a big florid round hand, each sinuous convolution an extravagant flourish, "To my handsome. Keep my babies safe. With love. Dora. xx" All the other photographs were of this woman. All monochrome. All of Dora Zygari.

I looked out over the empty sea. The mirrored door of the 1930's cupboard swung open sending another gentle waft of stale vinegar. The mirror caught my reflection, standing against the orange glow from the window. Who was he, my father? Had I really known the man at all?

I was still holding the photos when Zana came out of the bathroom. She sat down on Dad's neatly-made bed. "There's something going on. I can feel it."

"Me too. Look at these." I pointed to the crate of records. She pulled one out slowly, then another, then another.

"Who are you Lionel?" She murmured, "I mean, what's our connection?" She looked down at the discs were piled in her lap, "We've only known each other for two days. There's something weird, magical, isn't there, going on?"

"I don't know." I looked out the window at the sea, "It's like we're living inside that Ivor Novello musical. Doesn't it feel like that to you?"

"My grandmother had a poster for that performance. I found it in her attic." She smoothed the brown paper cover of the topmost record in her lap, "It's on my office wall."

"So...." My mind sought out the basics, retreating to the safety of fact, "we could be related...."

Zana interrupted. "I don't like living in someone else's story. I'm not singing." Her chin jutted. "Come on, let's go." Zana's voice was curt. She grabbed her coat. "We'll come back. Make sure you lock this flat." She turned half way down the stairs, "I forgot something. The fish and chip woman. She's got something for you." She went ahead down the stairs. She seemed to be angry with me.

The café was busy serving late afternoon teas, the owner turning the battered fish as we went in. Distracted, shouting orders in strident cockney, she took me to the back of the shop and quickly took down a scuffed paper bag, pushing it into my hands, following me back, almost pushing me out into the street. I was surprised the bag was so light.

"I'm Trudy. Pleased to meet you. Lovely man, your dad, but I'm glad you've come for it. Taking up a bit of space, it was, no offence mind." She looked at Zana, "Sad, isn't it?"

Zana was elbowed aside by a couple of hungry lads.

"Yes. But what did my father say?"

"Oh yes, thanks dear." Trudy turned away and yelled at a plump pale girl behind the counter. "Sharon! The Cod! Turn them or they'll burn!" She turned back. "Hopeless. Now, let's see, yes, he was very clear and particular. What was it? Oh yes." She stopped and looked at me closely. "You are his son, aren't you dear? He asked me to make sure."

I took out my wallet and showed Trudy my driving licence, reassuring myself. "Yes. I am Lionel Barty."

"That's lovely, no need really." She laughed, "I did promise him I would be careful. I mean, I didn't breathe a word to them others who came yesterday."

"Yesterday? Which others?"

"Not smart, they were. They had a key to the flat. Looked like Council people to me. They were asking me if there was anything else, but I said I didn't know, didn't breathe a word. It's a bit of a relief to tell you."

Zana looked at me, "What was it he said?"

"Oh, wait a minute." The fish and chip lady went to the till, "He was so old when he told me this, he may not have been all there, dear," She pulled out a piece of paper, an old wrinkled bill. She turned it over, reading her own writing.

"He said tell him, keep it safe. Someone will come. Open the seals." She looked up, "Those were his words exactly, just as he told me to say them." She handed the old bill to Zana. "You can keep it, dear, of course."

Inspector Brookhill was waiting on the kerb as we came out of Trudy's shop. My mind was clogging up. I had forgotten him.

"Mister Barty?" He was short, stocky, with white-flecked peppery hair and a reassuringly ordinary tone and manner. But his eyes were just a little beady, "I'm sorry I'm a bit late. Our men are coping with the crowds at the festival and I was delayed. Could we walk along for a little bit?" He looked at Zana, waiting for an introduction.

"This is Zana Sokoli, a friend."

Brookhill waited for a second, "Could we speak alone for a bit, Mr. Barty?"

"I'll wait upstairs. No," She changed her mind. "I'll go and try to see my grandmother for a bit, it's a short walk." She unrumpled the old bill and scribbled the address of the Home on the back and gave it to me.

Still clutching the paper bag, I followed Brookhill along the Esplanade towards the Spyglass Inn. A light fog had come in from the English Channel and twilight was not far away. The beach below the Esplanade was emptying, skeletons of lonely deckchairs left abandoned in small groups as the holidaymakers went back from the beach to their hotels for supper.

We reached the Spyglass and sat outside on the verandah, far away from the nearest drinkers. "Now, I don't want to alarm you unnecessarily, Mr. Barty."

"Lionel."

He coughed and produced a packet of cigarettes and lit one. Offered the pack to me, "No? OK, well it's this. It may be nothing, but I was in the Metropolitan Vice Squad, Soho District, before I came down here and it's to do with the way your father was found." He paused, "Face up, arms folded across his chest. Too neat. Didn't seem to be the way a man has a heart attack to me." He frowned, looked out across the sea into the thickening fog. "And there's something else, as well. We got a call. From an untraceable sim-card phone. Pay as you go. Telling us, the police, that Mr. Barty was dead." He looked at me. "That doesn't happen often in England, still less the Isle of Wight."

The fog was entering through my ears, damp, thick, cold, over the monotone rhythm of susurrating surf below us. I clutched the paper bag with both hands. I realised I was also still holding the Novello Programme, "What is it?"

Inspector Brookhill took a long drag on his cigarette, "Unless I've got it all wrong, your father had something that they believed had been stolen from them. Whether or not they have recovered what they were looking for, we'll probably never know. You'll never get anything out of them, even if we managed to catch them. I've asked for a post-mortem because I've seen it many times since they took over Soho's prostitution and drugs. It is the way that the Albanian mafia do it. It is stipulated in their ancient law. Their code. The Kanun of Lek Dukagjin."

"I'm afraid I'm lost, Inspector."

"In my opinion, Mr. Barty, Lionel, you may not only be lost, you may be in danger."

Brookhill looked over the foggy sea again. It was almost dark and the bright lights of the Esplanade had been lit. "And, if I'm right, I'm not sure we can protect you," He muttered, almost to himself. Then, remembering something, he looked at me, "Your girlfriend..."

"She's a friend, that's all."

"Have you known her for long?"

I had to admit that I had known her for only two days, although it felt longer. A lot longer.

"Sokoli is an Albanian name."

I told him that I knew that. That Zana had lived in England since she was eight.

"I would like to speak to her. Now, please."

An Irish folk band started up inside the bar of the Spyglass as we left. Inside, a blonde woman's pretty face at the bar turned and waved. If I wasn't feeling so paranoid, I wouldn't have believed she was waving at me.

21

Tirana

"This is, of course, totally confidential. I was never here and I don't want anything in writing. Just tell me what you know. Then destroy everything except for the tape and the discs. I'll take those with me. Understood?"

The lawyer looked at his client and nodded slowly, "I believe I have the whole story. I have some missing pieces from men who were in the Sigurimi in the 60s and 70s. In 2008 the Albanian parliament discussed opening the Sigurimi files, but the Socialist Party of Albania contested it. They may well have been destroyed." He went to the windows and closed the blinds on Perlat Rexhepi Street. "Sokoli was very hard to find. It took us weeks." He turned, "The new government is still trying to get the postal system to work. Up till now, it's been second green door in the third house south from the fishmonger, that sort of thing."

He had made sure that all the staff had left. The two sat in the smart wood-panelled conference room with the door locked. Neat rows of black and white pictures of old Tirana covered the walls, as carefully arranged and hung by an interior designer. A mountain highlander in traditional dress stared down at them, his felt skull cap, huge moustache, embroidered waistcoat, white kilt, sword and no less than three silver-embossed long-barrel flint-locks stuffed into his belt. Over his shoulder he carried a *tanchika* long rifle, a beautiful and deadly thing, a flint-lock with gold damascening, its barrel almost two metres long with engraved floral decoration, the silver butt-stock and forearm with brass panels, floral scrolls and red-paste inlaid roundels and punched copper rings. From another photo, three women looked at them in a set-piece studio photograph from about 1845 which had been taken by a German anthropologist. One looked startled and suspicious, the other two exhausted. Their faces, broad, high cheekboned, hardened, they wore the clothes of work – head-dress, thick wool felt undergarments, heavily embroidered tunics with long sleeves, leather slippers and thick dark wool socks. Round their waists and shoulders were thick-buckled belts hung with chains. On their backs, sacks of meat and skins of wine, and in their hands, baskets of bread and gourds of milk.

The lawyer's client stood up and approached the picture of the three women on the wall. He put out his hand and touched their faces, a light touch for so robust a man, almost a caress, "So that's where it all began."

"You know, life must have been excruciating for those women. We romanticise it now, but they were mule-slaves for life, couldn't so much as move, marry or moan without the permission of their fathers, husbands and brothers…who were all killing each other in endless blood-feuds." He stopped. "You know the mafia are after this too, don't you? You should be extra careful."

The lawyer nodded. "It is the Kanun of Lek Dukagjin. The mountain law. It still is. The mafia would think it was stolen from them." It was late and he wanted to go home. If the mafia were after it, he would find out. He would then, of course, sell the whole file to the mafia when his English client had gone back to the UK.

"Do you think you will ever find it?"

Audley Barty looked back at the faces of the women on the wall. "I believe I might have, but I still can't be sure."

22

Bonchurch

When Brookhill and I got to the Bonchurch Undermount Elderly Care Home it was dark and the Home was closed to visitors. Zana was sitting on a low bench next to Bonchurch pond, gazing at the ducks paddling under the willows. A full moon rode above the sea, casting black shadows and silver light, a bright path over the Channel towards France. Bonchurch was a dream landscape, a stage setting only a few minutes' walk along from Ventnor under the huge green might of the St. Boniface Down. Stone Victorian villas snuggled into the dark woodlands and rampant foliage. It was dead quiet. I could just see the radar tower masts on the top of the Down, still there, picked out like frosted salt-cellars against a thick mat of stars. I started to think of my father again, but one look at Zana's face showed her exhaustion. I was feeling done in too and I would need some food. I turned to Brookhill. "Can we leave it for today?" He nodded.

"Do you know anywhere we can stay? Where we can find something to eat?"

"There's the Bonchurch Inn, just up the road after the church. They'll do you." He reached into his pocket and pulled out his card, with a sideways glance at Zana, "Call me at any time in case of need. I'm only twenty minutes away."

Zana and I clambered up the steep road between high stone walls went up past an old church and found the Inn. It had once been the stables of the old Hotel next door (now private apartment flats) and was arranged around a courtyard, with the Tap and Restaurant set into one side and the kitchens on the other. Inside, the bar was wood-panelled and had a good fire going. A few locals were chuntering along about local politics, planning permissions and nothing much else apart from the huge amounts of mackerel which had been caught by one of them that morning. We ordered steak and salad and frites and Zana had wine and I sank into a pint of the local brown ale, nutty and deeply delicious. We ate in silence, we were both so tired. When they told us they only had one room spare, neither of us said anything. We just went along with it. I put the paper bag down on the dresser, tested my blood sugar and syringed my insulin into my leg. We got undressed to our underclothes and got into bed. There was a little bit of an atmosphere.

"We might be cousins." Zana murmured, as she rolled over away from me. She smelt nice and she had a very shapely figure with all dimples, curves and protuberances in just the right forms and places, but I felt protective of her. She was asleep almost immediately. I looked at her face and had a strange feeling because I realised that I was no longer seeing her as I had done. The desire to play my games had gone and instead I was with her in her game, totally. I pulled the cover over her, examining this new feeling, getting used to it. I felt comfortable, warm, stronger, protective. I was willing to give something if she needed it, make a sacrifice, without her asking. I didn't want to manipulate. I wanted to help her. This was new and it felt good.

I lay there until I could hear the locals saying good night and clattering out of the bar into the courtyard below. When their voices dissipated into the night, I gently got out of bed and crept across the floorboards to the dresser and opened the paper bag. The moonlight through the spaces around the window curtains was strong enough to see clearly. Inside the bag I found a black round metal cone-shaped canister with a rusty flat top. It was an old container for cleaning powder. Turning it in the light, I saw a black palm-print on a yellow circle underneath the legend, "*Cleans Dirty Hands*". Below the legend, in cream and red, was printed the name of the powder in much bigger letters. It was ZOG.

I quickly stifled my laughter. It wasn't the beer. The old bastard was playing a joke on me. Was it a coded message? Had he thought I had dirty hands? What had he thought of me?

I held the canister up and saw that the top had been soldered to the body. I shook out the paper bag and an envelope fell out. I could just make out that it was post-marked Tiranë 1967 and bore two Albanian postage stamps, one brown and one green, the first showing Lenin standing with his arm thrown forward in a posture of passionate oratory and, beside him, Joseph Stalin seated, from the side-view. The stamp celebrated 50 years of communism from 1917 to 1967. The second showed a family group under a statue of a soldier, the mother holding a baby girl whose arm was outstretched to give a bouquet of flowers to a saluting officer of the Sigurimi. A big blue pencilled cross had been drawn across the front of the envelope. Inside was a single sheet of cheap paper and on it was florid handwriting that I recognised.

"Jack, I am certain I am going to die. of love. Please keep the twins safe in the free world."

God knows how she had got it out past the censor. Maybe a bribe. It was obvious that the censor had not realised that the first sentence was the message and had overlooked the full stop, thinking it was no more than a sad billet-doux from a woman stuck behind the iron walls of her country to the foreign father of her children.

Twins? I looked across the room at Zana's head under the covers. Were we really related then? Her great-aunt my father's lover? What had I got myself into? And where were the twins now? Were they still alive?

I put the Zog canister and the envelope back in the bag and got into bed and managed to fall asleep.

23

I heard a sound. A smooth murmur seeping into my sleep, giving a gentle lift to my eye-lids. I opened my eyes. I could make out a thin line of gilded light between the closed curtains. Zana was standing by the window holding the canister. She was softly singing to herself, stroking the canister slowly, trance-like. Her voice had a yearning, a soft drone. She was naked. She gently put the canister down and then began to sway her hips in time to the rhythm of her soft song, turning in reverie in the slight moonlight, her hair dark over her face and the jutting splay of her breasts picked out above the dark of her belly. My hope that she was seducing me was stifled by her seclusion, her isolation in her own reverie, close and inviting but distant and unattainable, lost in her dream, making it heresy for me to move or speak.

I closed my eyes. Her sound was fluid and tranquil, the tones smooth, forming a thread, twisting, suggesting other notes, shining inflamed beads and darker moist shades on a string, deep sadness and wistful rapture woven with the languish of joy, creating other tunes behind and underneath, other beads, other strings, voices playing in my head until my thought was full. And with the fullness came an understanding. The soft sounds twined and wrapped and folded, a tickled caress at the underbelly of my mind. My thoughts evaporated, bringing a perfect stillness, like a trout hypnotised under the dark bank of a moonlit river. I let the weight of the song carry me deeper into the warm ripples of my understanding, each little wave spreading outward, catching the moon, as the surface of things softly evaporated, hearing the voice of the water and of the earth and the moonlight, seeing everything that had gone before me up-stream and knowing that with a flick of a fin I would follow the water current downstream. The sounds carried me to her core, the tender essence of her femininity. I was suspended, knowing that if her bidding came, I would follow it.

24

"You need a shower." Not the most romantic opening to the day from the beautiful girl beside me. I thought about the shadow who had danced and sung in the night. Was it real? Perhaps she had dreamt. It was a sensitive memory and something had passed between us without touching. The memory of my swollen erection was still there. But I said nothing, just watched her, awed.

Both having showered, my blood sugar tested and insulin taken, she having changed into clean jeans and t-shirt, I told Zana about the Zog canister and Dora's letter. She took the canister and read the letter. She was subdued.

Over breakfast in the bar, she murmured, "You know, I feel like we are shackled to a chain. When we move, the chain unwinds a bit more. Then a bit more. But we still can't see the hidden capstan behind the bulkhead." She gazed across the empty tables. A van drew up outside and a man came in with some deliveries. "Who were the twins?"

"I never knew anything about any twins. They would have been my half-siblings." I looked at her. "And it would mean that we're related, wouldn't it? We would be sort of cousins." I tried not to show it, but my new warm feelings were making it impossible. I didn't like the idea of Zana being my cousin. But then I remembered that it was perfectly legal for cousins to have a relationship.

"Mmm." She didn't pursue it and changed the subject. "It all started with that session at the Institute. A catalyst. I have a feeling that somehow it triggered a process which is still going on in real life. That all my forebears are standing in a hidden line, looking at me, waving me on as they slowly turn the capstan and let the chain loose."

"Would you cut it if you could?"

She looked at me slowly, her hazel eyes had a lucid glitter despite the feeble morning light in the bar. "No. I want to find who's turning the capstan."

Zana stood and went across to the young woman at the bar. "I wonder, please, if you could lend us a pair of pliers?"

Back in the room, I held the canister down on the dresser with both hands and turned it slowly round while Zana carefully cut the solder and pulled the lid off with the pliers. It felt vaguely indecent, like violating an heirloom. The lid finally came off.

Inside there was an aluminium foil packet. Zana took a pair of nail scissors from her bag and carefully snipped at the top of the aluminium.

Inside there were just two small tightly-wound spools of magnetic recording tape. Nothing else.

Zana held them delicately in each hand and looked at them, a long slow whistle on her lips, quickly suppressed. "I know a place in London who might be able to play these," She turned away, "and transfer them to digital if we find anything." She put the tapes carefully back in the tin canister and then put the canister in her bag.

She turned back. "Do you agree? I'll keep them safe."

"Fine by me," I said. "Shall we still go to see your Grandmother?"

"Very quickly," She said, "Then I have to get back. After all, I have work to do for your uncle."

25

The Bonchurch Undermount Elderly Care Home was approached by a tunnel through the rock. A sign said *"For Residential, Respite and Day Care – Experienced in Care of Dementia with Personal Privacy and Dignity."*

The tunnel gave out on a sweeping gravel drive and there, a substantial Victorian Mansion in the style of a French chateau set its proud face against the sea, its tended lawns stretching down to the beach beyond, the blue sea water stretching back to the horizon.

We were shown into a huge and ornate ballroom panelled in dark, rather forbidding, heavy mahogany.

"Her recent memory is virtually non-existent, as you know," The nurse said as if reciting from a manual, "But long-term memory is a little better, if sporadic. We'll bring her down in a moment." She left us with a professional smile.

Zana and I sat in a corner on leather armchairs. A thin, nerdy young man in a tweed jacket came in and moved to a piano in the opposite corner. "Good morning", he called across cheerfully, then with that English way of having to add another unnecessary phrase for good measure so as not to be too curt, "The acoustics in here are excellent."

He opened the piano and trilled through the first few bars of *Oh, What a Beautiful Morning*. He seemed friendly enough. I stood up and walked across, watching him take some sheet music from a leather music case. He looked up and smiled short-sightedly at me, "Whom have you come to visit?" I noticed his meticulous grammar.

"Zana Zygari."

"Oh yes, a nice lady. When she sings with us she still can hit the notes, you know." He smiled, "The others can be a little bit jealous. They can get terribly petulant, as you probably know. Is she a relative?"

Good question. I couldn't say, "maybe", so I said "yes."

Zana came over, "Are you a music therapist?"

The young man bowed from his piano stool. "We don't start for another 30 minutes. I like to warm up." He was obviously struck by Zana's good looks. He looked down at the piano keys, blushing. "When it comes to dementia, music therapy is one of the most successful interventions. It's a means of communication where the function of language has become very challenging or lost. Music is pre-verbal, predating the ability for language, processed by many different parts of the brain - rhythm, pitch, and melody and are all processed differently."

Zana was smiling at him, aware of her effect. I began to recognise a fellow Aspergic (in him, not her). It was his obsession.

"The emotions activate the limbic system. The arousal is in the brain stem and the dynamic registers in the basal ganglia. It shows how basic and primeval sound is to humans. Musical memory. I see it when a patient remembers all the words to a song yet rarely speaks or can put a coherent sentence together. It's a catalyst for memory, for reminiscence..."

I took out the *Glamorous Night* from my bag, "Do you know this?"

"Oh yes, Novello." He squinted at me, "Which song would you like me to do?"

Zana looked at me. She knew what I was up to, "Could you play the last one, *The Girl I Knew*, when we give you the nod?"

"My favourite. Yes, of course."

The door opened and an old lady was wheeled in in a wheelchair. As she was pushed closer across the room, the sun came out of the clouds outside and bright rays of light filled the room, picking out even the darkest corners. She was lit up and she was an extraordinary sight. She was skeletally thin under a yellow aertex blanket and her hair was teased straight up on top of her head in about ten or twelve inches of frizzy dark grey wire wool, held together by a blue velvet bow, looking much like a hay-sheaf stack left in a field after the others had been gathered up. Underneath, her dark eyes watched us like a distracted crow. She was holding a silver-handled magnifying glass, peering through it at an old lottery scratch-card from which all of the numbers had been scratched off, over and over again. She was muttering to herself in a language I didn't recognise.

The Nurse applied the brakes to the wheelchair. "Now Missus Zygari, here's your visitors. You be a good girl for me, won't you?" She smiled at us, "Call me if you need anything, won't you? If you would like to stay longer after the Music Therapy begins, we can find you another room." She looked over at the pianist, "Keep it down, Eric, won't you?"

Eric waved at her from the piano.

Zana reached for her grandmother's hand. "Grandma? It's Zana...." She gently held her hand and stroked it softly.

I remembered that this was the woman who had had the strength to persuade the British government to send in a group over the Yugoslavian border to rescue her grand-daughter all those years ago from a country iron-bound by a cold-war dictator. Who had travelled to Vienna to collect her. This woman's eyes now stared at Zana in blank puzzlement. She jerked her hand away and took up the magnifying glass and scratched at the scratch-card furiously, "I can never win," She whispered, "I'll never win."

"I'm sure you can. If you keep trying." Zana spoke softly, but her eyes were strangely hard. "If we keep trying."

Unbidden, the first piano notes of *The Girl I Knew* floated across the room. Eric had taken a quiet initiative, probably hoping to please Zana, I thought.

The old woman reached out to touch Zana's face. "Dora. You were always the pretty one weren't you, Dora?"

Eric's thin voice began crooning. *"I sit before my mirror and stare, the girl I knew no longer is there, the girl I knew could never be false to you...."*

"You are still very beautiful, Grandmother…"

"Yes. You were the pretty one, the one up on the stage, the one everyone wanted. But I could sing too you know." There was a touch of petulance in the old lady's voice, and then pity, "You were led, it was so easy to lead you by the nose, pretty one," then disgust. "You were a fool to go back."

She picked up the scratch card, crumpled it into a ball and threw it in Zana's face. "You gave them away Dora. You gave them away."

She stopped. The old woman crumpled in her seat. Her face had softened. Lines in her brow smoothed out as she relapsed. The memories had vanished, the accusation gone. She looked up at me. The heat of clear recognition made her eyes come alive again. "You always said women had to manipulate to survive, didn't you, my friend?"

Who did she think I was?

The old lady smiled to herself, comforted by her new thought, "But you were always my friend."

Zana was staring at me. I started to shake my head, but Zana quickly put her hand on mine, miming to stop me, "Yes, he is your friend and always has been. He's a very good friend."

The old lady reached up, hand shaking, pointing at my face, "Audley. Yes Audley, we agreed, but it was because of you that I killed them all. It was my fault." She burst into tears, "It was all my fault."

The nurse came in to try to calm her. She asked us to leave. As we made for the door, I waved goodbye to Eric who was still warbling at the piano.

Zana walked straight outside to the entrance and stood in the sun. "Do you have a cigarette?"

"I don't smoke."

"Shit." She was tight, tense, coiled up. "So you were right." She hit her hand against the stone arch of the entrance, "I've never heard her say that before." She walked around in small circles, breathing heavily, her neck clenched. Then, suddenly, she asked me to wait there at the front entrance and went back inside. She disappeared for about eight minutes. I thought she had gone to the toilet, but she came back with a hardback book, scuffed and well-thumbed. She handed it to me. "I had to search for it in her things." It was called, *King Zog: Self-Made Monarch of Albania* by Jason Tomes.

I opened it and on the fly-leaf was written, "To Zana. In condolence and with heartfelt apology. Audley."

"She will never read it again," Zana shrugged, "But you won't find the answer in it." Downcast, she made for the tunnel. "Neither will I. And I probably never will."

26

Zana stayed quiet all the way until the train pulled into Petersfield station. We had found two seats with difficulty because the train was packed full of returning festival-goers, noisily talking about the acts they had seen, comparing bands and singers, bemoaning the need to go back to work the next day.

Zana had picked up some discarded pink pages from an abandoned section of *The Financial Times* and seemed to be engrossed in an article contained inside them. She threw it down and gazed out of the window at the lush wide green spaces as we went through the Meon valley with a hill-top church, its woodlands and meadows. When she had looked away from the window at me, her glances were troubled.

"So. Lionel? I know Audley Barty, of course. I've met him. Jack's brother. She thought you were him. So they already knew each other. It's in the book I gave you."

"He might have looked like me when he was younger." This didn't cast any light, of course. Then I had a simple and obvious idea. "Why don't you just go to Albania and find your father? After all, Zana, he's the only one who can give you the answer you're looking for. It's a small country and someone must know if he's still alive and where to find him."

"I could. Of course I could. But…" Her expression darkened, "Grandma always insisted that he had betrayed my mother. Just now, she might have been confused, rambling, got it wrong, forgotten the truth. If he did betray my mother, I don't want to meet him ever. What would it achieve? I'd rather try and forget all about it."

"Why otherwise would she have men sent across the border to get you?"

"Mmm." Zana looked at her feet, struck by a recollection, looked up at me sharply, "But then, of course I only met Audley because he 'phoned me…. He sought me out…." She looked full of suspicion, her voice rising, "Why?"

"Why don't we ask him?"

She looked at me as if I was a simpleton. "He could have told me when I met him. Why the subterfuge? Why play games with me? With you? What does he want that he couldn't get without us being involved? That he can't disclose in a straightforward way?"

"You mean something that only we could find?"

"Christ! Of course! That's so funny!" Zana's eyes dilated and she started to choke. She snorted and her mouth opened, her shoulders shaking, as she tried to hold her hand to her mouth as a scratchy mewling rasping cough began to unwind from her throat. I stood up and held her close to me, thumping her back, looking around the carriage at the alarmed faces of the other passengers as she let splutters of deep snorting grunts into my shoulder. The coughs and grunts became a panting chortle and then a full-blown shrieking yelping laugh. She fell back into her seat, convulsed, her eyes red with tears…

A dark young woman with tattoos and several ear-rings through her nose handed me a bottle of water and I opened it and pushed it at Zana. "Zana, Zana drink this…." Zana took the bottle and drank, the convulsion passing, her breathing getting softer. Soon, she just lay in her seat, gazing at me, "Thank you." She said simply.

"What is it?"

"Sorry. I haven't, I think, ever laughed before….Never," A shadow crossed her face, "I suppose I will have to get used to it. To this new sound." She gazed at me. "Can you believe it?"

"You poor thing," I said, "I am sorry that your laugh has such a bitter…."

She was looking at me as if I was really stupid. She reached in her bag and took out the tin canister. "It's got to be these, these old magnetic tapes, hasn't it?" She was not speaking to me anymore, but to herself, "Hidden by Jack, your father, but belonging to Dora my great-aunt. Why?" She looked at me, her voice quiet but her face a mask of bleak chill, her eyes wet. "Have you played with me, Lionel?" She opened her eyes wide with accusation, "Are you Tom Rakewell or Nick Shadow?" She grimaced, teeth clenched, "Or are you just a fool?"

She wasn't making sense. I didn't know Tom Rakewell or Nick Shadow. I stood up and went down the carriage and called Twilda from the train.

"Twilda? It's Lionel." My voice in my head was rattled, tremulous, "I need to speak to Audley in private, please. It's urgent. Where is he now and when's he back?"

I could hear Twilda start to answer, but then the mobile signal went.

I went back to my seat. Zana's face was tight, wrenched, all traces of humour gone. "Have you played with us?" Tears of hurt were rimpling her eyes. "Used me?"

"No." I reached out to her, "Not me."

"You're either with me or not, Lionel. What is it going to be?"

"But Audley is my uncle….."

She pulled her hand away, grabbed her 'phone and bag and went down the carriage towards the toilet.

I looked around the carriage. The dark young woman with tattoos was gulping from a lager can, eyes down. A blond man with startling blue eyes who faced her, slumped in his seat in a kaftan and muddy shorts who had put his feet on the seat beside her, eyed me with a kind of sympathy, undecided whether to say anything. I avoided his gaze and toyed with the few sheets of *The Financial Times* which Zana had discarded, my mind on Audley. The pink pages held the usual stuff – companies over-paying their directors, boardroom disputes, take-over evaluations and then a tedious article giving a report by a department of the European Commission. It concerned a report by a European Commission investigatory committee that Pharcutrix Chemicals (pharmaceuticals, electronics and high-end sound-recording equipment) was in fact a money-laundering outfit, funded mainly by Albanian marijuana and other drugs.

The train slowed after Petersfield and came to a stop just before a bridge. In the undergrowth by the railway I saw a movement in the hedges and a dark, thin head appeared between leaves, its ears torn and mottled with disease, its grimy russet hair matted with black streaks. The fox stopped still and looked up at the train. Its narrowed eyes searched along the carriage until they met mine and then passed on, slowly studying the travellers' faces, but then returned as if in recognition and then stopped, fixed on my gaze. All sounds went quiet except for a slight hiss from the carriage brakes. The fox was nearly dead. I felt his bleakness. We held each other's gaze until the carriage suddenly jerked forward with a crashing pull of the engine and the fox leapt back, turned and disappeared into the bushes.

Zana came back much later as we were drawing into Waterloo station. She must have gone to sit at the other end of the train. At Waterloo, we disembarked and stood at the gate. "I'll tell you what's on the two tapes and if we have any success," She said curtly, "You know where to find me."

"You know, Zana, I always wanted to…"

She held up her hand. "Don't." It was probably a trick of the light, maybe just the crowds, but there was a row of people standing behind her. I was aware of them, and felt them, all looking at me without expression, much as waxwork statues in a museum. Uncle Audley at the front, then Old Zana, then Dora, then Jack, Zana's mother, an old man with a moustache and a stick, all of them all the way back down the line. Right at the back was a man in uniform. I squinted, trying to make out the man at the back. He wore a moustache, like Adolf Hitler's and Charlie Chaplin's, with little curlicues, and wore a white military uniform encrusted with medals in various star-shapes, gold sash and epaulettes, and held a ceremonial sword with both hands. He was tall, but of medium build. Dark hair parted to the left over a receding hairline, he looked at me along the line between us. He was smoking a cigarette and I could smell the Turkish tobacco, its smoke floating towards me over the intervening shoulders. His expression was not unkind. It was more disappointed, perplexed and slightly hurt, the expression of a man alone on a platform, who had missed a train and didn't know when the next one was coming, or if one ever would.

I reached in my pocket and swallowed a glucose tablet. The line of waxworks evaporated amongst the crowd. Zana raised her hand again. "You won't forget me, will you?" She actually smiled and then turned away from me. It was, I think, the first time I had seen her smile.

I stayed at the gate and watched Zana walk away. For a short time after her slight figure had disappeared, I could still see the top of her dark head going the opposite way against the crush of the evening crowd.

I never saw her again.

Part Four

Truth

27

London

Zana's complete disappearance wasn't evident to me for a bit. She didn't call me so after a few days I called her phone, but it didn't ring. I didn't have her address. I checked the phone books, the internet, everything. But there was nothing. Nothing at all.

I got a call from Twilda Tonlinson from Audley's office in Mayfair. Her master wanted to see me. It was urgent. To explain things, she said.

Audley met me at his home in Canary Wharf, one of those smart flats converted from an old warehouse overlooking the river. Dek was there. I won't bore you with exclamation marks, my feelings about that or the dawning of my realisation that I had been set up by my relative and my friend. I'll stick to the facts, it's easier for me, you see.

Audley had got his boat ready, Dek took the wheel and we set off down the Thames towards the sea.

Audley was a lot harder than I had ever seen him. He had used me, yes. In a nutshell, he explained that he was MI6, and that Dek and Brookhill were with him. Zana had disappeared. He had found out that she had emptied one of the trust accounts a few days ago when she had reached her thirtieth birthday. He was one of the Trustees. Twilda Tonlinson was the other. The money was Old Zana's and had originally been a gift to her and her sister from King Zog. Over time and constant re-investment, it was a huge sum of money and Zana had taken almost all of it, with a tiny bit of signature-forgery thrown in.

"But why didn't you just tell me about all this before it all started?" I felt injured by his clandestine distrust.

"I was wrong. I wanted to see if I could put the occult into practical use." He looked across at the Tower of London as we passed under Tower Bridge, "I had no other way of seeing if the tapes still existed. It was my last chance. Jack would never tell me if they existed or where they were. He'd kept his word to Dora, hidden them. I sent some people round to the flat after he died but they couldn't find anything, although you'd never know they had been in."

We moored off the Greenwich Bank and Dek went into the galley and prepared some lunch for us all. He didn't look sheepish at all. Just very professional.

We sat at the table on the stern, the Royal Observatory on the starboard side as we swung at anchor. "It's better out here where nobody can hear and we're out of range of recording equipment. So Lionel, I'm going to tell you the whole story."

"Albania is a strange country and Zog was a strange man. Some saw him as a joke, others as a manipulative brigand, others as a hero who had been sorely betrayed. Anyway, Zog started off life as the son of an ordinary tribal chief, but was unusually highly-educated by the Ottomans in Constantinople. He basically plotted his way to the top, keeping the other brigands at bay, and declared himself king of Albania. He took lots of money from the Italians in return for serial promises of co-operation. When the Italians invaded in 1939 and took over, Zog was deposed and basically ran away with his six sisters, his heavily pregnant wife Geraldine (who gave birth on a mattress in the mountains) and, of course, Dora and Zana Zygari amongst others who collectively were called "King Zog's Circus" in the English press."

"He was, of course, a womaniser and Zana is his illegitimate grand-daughter by Old Zana. He looted public funds from the Albanian treasury and took with him a bright red Mercedes (which had been given to him by Adolf Hitler in happier times as a wedding present) and trunks and trunks of money, gold and diamonds and other valuables. Desperate at the outbreak of the

Second World War, when the Germans reached the English Channel on 20th May 1939, Zog fled Paris. He filled six cars and a lorry and joined six million French refugees going south-west. When Bordeaux was bombed, he went south to Bayonne – on the advice of one Ian Fleming of British Naval Intelligence, of whom you may have heard. At St. Jean de Luz there were British merchant ships evacuating refugees and he managed to persuade the captain of the liner, *SS Ettrick*, to find room for royalty. But the captain omitted to mention that he wouldn't be taking his baggage. His circus had forgotten the loot on shore in the panic and confusion and he had to go back and get it by speedboat before the ship sailed for England at dawn."

"Throughout the war, the British government kept Zog in warm storage. Polite but distant, they refused to meet him. Eventually, as Queen Geraldine and her young boy were terrified of the Blitz, King Zog's circus left for a large country house in quiet, leafy Sunninghill in Berkshire and then moved to a Queen Anne mansion in Henley-on-Thames, where the sisters and the Queen began a secret feud for his affections while Zog played them all along. Bored with life in the country, as the World War raged in the cities across Europe and in most other parts of the world, Dora resumed her singing career and Zana managed it for her, more for something to do than anything else."

I tried to interrupt, but Audley asked me to hear him out. "Dear Boy, you'll never understand unless I tell you the whole story from beginning to end." He took a sip of wine and carried on. Dek was smoking a cigarette, head leant back in the sun which had broken out above Greenwich.

"Back in the Balkans, Tito sent a band of comrades over to Albania in 1941 to stir up support and the Albanian Communist Party was established in 1941. It was led by one Enver Hoxha – the future communist dictator who would hold the country in his grip for 40 years after the end of the war."

"After the Italians surrendered in 1943 and switched sides, the British sent over fifty Liaison Officers into Albania. I was one of them."

"We found a bunch of clans, all predominantly interested in profit, and all at each other's throats. We trusted none of them and they didn't trust us or each other. But eventually, we gave then rifles and Hoxha's communist partisans started to win what had become a civil war."

"Having become an irrelevance in England, Zog left Buckinghamshire on 11th February 1946 and sailed from Liverpool to Egypt with his wife, son and dwindling circus the next day. Dora and Zana Zygari chose to stay behind and found a house in Sussex."

"Then, two British destroyers hit communist mines and sank in the Corfu Channel in October 1946 with the loss of over 40 lives. We decided to try clandestine operations to overthrow Hoxha. In 1949 I and some others went to see Zog in Cairo. Our first infiltrators went ashore on the night of 3rd October 1949." Audley coughed, "They were ambushed within hours and killed. It got worse. We were in cahoots with the CIA and on New Year's Eve, 1953, because of Kim Philby's betrayal, our men were caught and shot by Hoxha's secret police."

"But what happened to Dora?" I asked.

"Well, this is it, isn't it Dear Boy? You see Zog didn't drink alcohol, apart from occasional champagne and, whilst he smoked about 200 cigarettes a day, he never got drunk. So when he took me aside in Cairo and told me about Zana and Dora Zygari, I was only vaguely interested until he told me that they, between them, knew traditional songs which had been known for over 500 years. He told me that the sounds of these songs had been adapted by the women over the centuries of conflict, so that when sung by two women in different parts – two parts – in carefully timed counterpoint, it produced a variable harmonic."

"This harmonic would create a different, high sound which had a strangely compulsive effect on the male human brain. He had tried to listen to it himself and said it was very, very pleasant. He confided in me that the tension created by the first notes was almost sexual and the release on the last notes, as the harmonic modulated and changed, felt definitely sexual. A bit like an orgasm, it altered the hormonal balance, he thought, releasing tension and calming aggression and anxiety. The problem was that no-one could hear it. It – the harmonic - was beyond the range of the human ear.

"I filed a report of the conversation with MI6, but they pooh-poohed it as superstitious nonsense spouted by a man who was now known to be little more than a joke, shacked up in Cairo with nothing better to think about. The reason I took an interest was much later, in the 1960s, I had read a report, lifted from an internal radio message, that Hoxha was thinking of beginning a series of secret experiments on something to do with the ear in Tirana."

Audley paused, his matter-of-fact tone had disappeared. "So I tracked Old Zana down. She was still living in Sussex. I asked her about it and she confirmed what Zog had said. She told me that the songs had been devised by the mountain women to control their proud, violent, lazy, brigand husbands and brothers and sons. "Women don't make war," she said, "and the men treated us as slave animals." She said that the harmonic seemed to tap into the men, making them more docile and controllable. She didn't know how it worked, of course, but very few women had the training or the voice."

She asked me to help her. She had fled with the Zog circus, thinking that they would return in a few weeks. She had had to leave her daughter behind in Albania in a village high up in the mountains. She prayed every day that the daughter was still alive. She would be grown up and could have been married, but of course she had no news because Hoxha had locked the country up. In return she would tell me everything she knew.

"I promised to help. We sent a group through Tito's Yugoslavia to the Albanian border and got the last child of the family out." He shrugged, "That, of course, was your Zana."

"My Zana? She's certainly not that…" I felt a sharp pain.

Audley looked at me with a strange sympathy, held that expression for a moment, then coldly went back to his story. "The Sigurimi found out about it. Tragically, Old Zana's decision to save the child and our cross-border raid made Hoxha and the Sigurimi certain that there was something in the legend. They stepped up the experiments. Zana's father tried to save his wife by co-operating with the secret police as long as his wife would not be harmed. They agreed. They could see the value in propaganda, if only they could isolate it – recreate the harmonic on tape. It would have been incredibly effective, if they had succeeded." Audley paused, "It will be incredibly effective. When we find it. Now, in the days of instantaneous global communication networks. Anyway, they lured Dora Zygari back."

"I found out that Jack, my brother, your father, had known Dora Zygari during the war. The trouble was, he fell in love with her – a junior radar corporal in Ventnor at the time of the D-Day operation, when Ventnor and Shanklin were very important positions – for the Channel petrol pipeline ran under the sea to the French coast to supply the British and American troops – and, of course for the radar station on the top of the Ventnor Downs. Why had Dora returned his affections? Christ knows, he had always been a fairly miserable bugger, but he was a tremendous flirt. But Old Zana said that Jack had succeeded in capturing the harmonic on tape, recording Dora singing first one part and then the other on a captured German Magnetophon recorder in the basement of the Shanklin Theatre. He then played both in synchronicity and recorded the result."

Audley looked at me, his tone lowered. "The tapes were the only existing recording of this secret harmonic in the entire world."

"But Jack had given his word to Dora. He told me he had destroyed them. He lied to me." Audley watched me, "So I had to use you."

"After all, I was a trustee of Old Zana's estate. I planted a flat-mate in with Zana at her flat. I lured you onto that course. I put Dek in the boat beside you. Sent Brookhill down to keep an eye on you. All that effort," He looked at me with grim recrimination, "The good thing is that it worked. The bad thing is ….."

"What happened to Zana's parents?"

"Well, her father is still alive. He's very old now."

"And?"

Audley looked away. He considered the façade of the Royal Observatory for quite a long time before he coughed and looked back. "The tragedy of it, Lionel, is that, despite the efforts of her father who was put in the aluminium mines when the experiment failed, Zana's mother was taken out, denounced as a fraud, accused of betraying the dictatorship, incriminated as a Christian and…"

"Shot?"

He nodded. "Old Grandma Zana never forgave herself. By saving her grand-daughter, she had sacrificed her own daughter. She has lived in purgatory ever since. The only way she could cope with the guilt was to make up stories, blame Zana's father. Now her memory is going or has gone, thank God, she can have some peace…the dementia is her salvation."

"Zana thinks that her father killed her mother, that he was some mindless egoistic state policeman who thought only of his career and believed he had been betrayed by his wife. But no. He did his utmost to save her. He actually volunteered for the mines to make them promise to save her. He was betrayed by his own people."

I too studied the Royal Observatory for a few moments. "I know where the tapes are." I mumbled.

29

Audley listened to me carefully as I slowly told him the story of Zana. When I finished and took another gulp of the wine which had now gone straight to my head, his reaction was, I thought, not a little harsh, given the circumstances. "So you blew it."

My annoyance at his unfairness was made dangerously combustible by the wine, "If you'd told me about this before, it might have turned out alright. Why didn't you just tell me? And I wouldn't….Do you know where she is?"

"Maybe, Dada, maybe." He looked doubtful. "Maybe I can find her for you."

I broke in, "Was Inspector Brookhill making it up about the mafia in Ventnor?"

"Brookhill gets a little bit imaginative sometimes. No, Jack wasn't murdered. The Albanian mafia wouldn't kill anyone in their home. That would contravene their Kanun, their law. I wouldn't have killed him. He was my brother. The bad thing is….."

I interrupted him again, "The good thing is that there seems to be a balance of natural justice in these things and by a quirk the tapes have landed back in the hands of their true owner.

After all your meticulous planning and contrivance, the songs went to the true inheritor. It's karma."

"Karma, unfortunately, has at least two sides and at least two sharp edges. Do you think she'll get in touch with you?" Audley sounded plaintive. He wasn't used to defeat, as he saw it.

"What were *you* going to use it for?"

"Anything. Anti-terrorist propaganda mainly." He was as vague as that, "Advertising…. After all, it would have been worth many, many, many millions….." He ended sadly.

"Maybe she has a better use. After all, the male brain is a dangerous thing isn't it? It has to be manipulated, as all women know, if the village, the country, the human race, is to survive."

30

I walked along the embankment. Dek was there. Over the next few months, we made friends again. But the whole business would never fade in my mind, it wouldn't wear off, and I couldn't forget her, as Zana had said.

Uncle Audley was propitiatory, giving me his constant attention. This was nice for a bit, but increasingly I found myself wanting to be alone with the Dora Zygari records and the Ivor Novello CD I had bought and a stiff drink. I played them over and over again, just as my father had done, nursing his misery and his memory of the woman he had loved. As I did now. *"I sit before my mirror and stare, the girl I knew no longer is there, the girl I knew could never be false...."*

I kept the old crumpled paper bill from the fish and chip lady and pinned it on the wall. *"Someone will come. Open the seals."* My father's words. And it was Zana he was talking about. I knew that now. Someone will come. And I hadn't seen her pain or been able to help her and she had run away.

It was about six months later that BBC News told of an Ofcom report which had come out with concerns about subliminal advertising released from an unknown source which had spread across the world and which had been only partially analysed. It was known to have a very curious and compulsive effect on the male population and further investigations were continuing. What was of concern to advertisers globally, and perceived to be dangerous, was that when it was used, any idea associated with it in the advertising or propaganda would be accepted without question. For instance, men were known not to enjoy shopping but sales of male-oriented goods had rocketed, so it was very good for the economy. The effect was not physically harmful and seemed to counteract the overbearing effect of the hormone testosterone.

It did not affect women. Women didn't need to be persuaded to shop.

Nobody could figure out how it worked.

I put the bottles aside (not quite *over* the side), hauled myself out of bed and decided to write about it to try and get it out of my system. Then I published this book. Audley was upset and gave me the cold-shoulder for a bit because of it, but I did it as a way of exorcising my demon, a way of sending a message out into the darkness, I suppose, hoping that Zana would read it and learn the whole story and get in touch. But I didn't hear from Zana and in the end my pain and remorse did wear off. Loss was replaced by a more positive thing and I could admire her beauty and sadness without having to, well, try to win or own her, I suppose. Zana was a beautiful memory and I genuinely hoped she had found a way of living with herself and her legacies. I hoped she had learned to laugh.

I did get a job in the end. It was in the West End and I rather enjoyed being back at work, being with people who seemed free of turmoil (although you can never really tell with most people, I had learnt). The musicians themselves though, the clients, always seemed to be in a state of turmoil.

Then one day, in the office, surrounded by the members of a band who had just had a number one album and their rather unpleasant manager, my 'phone shook itself on mute, but I was busy in the meeting and it was only an hour later that I could open the message from an unknown number. It contained quite a long video. At first, I thought it must be a promo from one of the record companies, but when I looked at it, it looked more like an amateur home movie. Then I added an Epilogue.

EPILOGUE

High Albania

The video was jumpy, but had sound, and showed a uniformed driver with a black peaked cap driving what looked to be an expensive car. It showed Nana Teresa Airport and a figure stepping down the stairs from what looked like a private jet. The person was slim, dark, well-dressed in a dark-grey charcoal suit. A hat and dark glasses. Slightly theatrical, maybe, but otherwise unexceptional.

Then the inside of the car - equipped with a sliding section which blocked the driver's view of the passenger, then dust and countryside. Then higher passes far up in the ravines, rutted narrow roads and dust covering the shining paintwork.

The video showed a small village called Krasta, then a track even higher and then through a pine forest along the edge of a waterfall to a tiny group of mountain smallholdings perched on the edge of a steep crevasse.

The driver had obviously stopped the car. A line of smoke formed a straight line from one of the chimneys, unbroken by breeze in the windless silence of the thin mountain air. Beyond the smallholding there were snow-capped peaks shining in the sunlight.

A muslim woman with a head scarf and shawl emerged from a door and stopped, shading her eyes, looking down at the car. She called inside and a man shuffled out in a threadbare woollen overcoat, leaning on two sticks, looking down at the car and the photographer. He went inside and came out again with an old Kalashnikov rifle and stood waiting, leaning against the door-frame, the rifle held at an angle downwards, parallel to his right-hand stick. A couple of pigs and a goat behind the wicket fence stopped eating and looked up expectantly. I could hear chickens squawk and cackle from a wooden coop. The passenger opened the rear door and got out, closing it with a gentle thud. The passenger then walked slowly, rather gingerly, up the dirt track to the stone huts towards the couple.

I saw the passenger reach the fence and take off the hat and dark glasses and face the old man who squinted and pulled at his moustache and then slowly, so slowly, as recognition crossed the threshold of his mind and replaced disbelief, lowered the rifle, tears running silently down the crevices in his lined cheeks as he went down on his knees.

In the still air, the video had easily caught what the old man had mumbled. All he had said was, "You are like your mother."

The passenger turned towards the camera. It was Zana. She looked happy in her quiet way. She had come to rest at last. She put her finger to her lips and then gave me a small wave. The video stopped. She had found what she needed. Her answer.

It made me feel proud of myself.

<u>Acknowledgements</u>

I would like to thank the following for their (mostly unknowing) inspiration or support or sources:

Philippa Lubbock of Life Alignment and Family Constellations;

The College of Psychic Studies, London.

Robert Elsie, author of many books on Albania and Albanian culture.

Paul Siebertz - Albanien und die Albanesen, Vienna 1910, Translated from the German by Robert Elsie.

Eve Kosofsky Sedgwick - Between Men: English Literature and Male Homosocial Desire (1985) and Jane Austen and the Masturbating Girl (1991).

Dr. Dessislava Dragneva - Conceptions of Decay in Czech and Bulgarian Nationalism (2005), University of London.

Jason Tomes – "King Zog: Self-Made Monarch of Albania" The History Press. ISBN-13: 978-0750944397

Eno Koço – "Albanian Urban Lyric Song in the 1930s" The Scarecrow Press. ISBN 0-8108-4889-9

Gjergj Fishta. The Highland Lute (Lahuta e Malcís) Translated from the Albanian by Robert Elsie & Janice Mathie-Heck. ISBN 1-84511-118-4

Extracts from Wikipaedia -
http://en.wikipedia.org/wiki/Italian_invasion_of_Albania
http://en.wikipedia.org/wiki/Wikipedia:Text_of_Creative_C
ommons_Attribution-ShareAlike_3.0_Unported_License.